He snatched his crossbow and stepped out of the doorway into the clearing. He appeared to look around him uncertainly for a moment or two, then he began to limp away, dragging one leg badly. . . .

Diarmid went faster, weaving from side to side, tongues of flame leaping up all around him. His jacket was smoldering. There was a lick of flame on his trews. The ground exploded into flame right in front of him. He fell, rolling over, his clothes on fire.

Rura screamed—and had just enough sense to tear her gaze away from the writhing figure and look at the chopper. Maybe it was in range, maybe it wasn't. But she couldn't let Diarmid burn like that. She ran out of the house towards him. He saw her.

"Now!" he screamed. "Damn you, now!"

She raised the rifle, maximum range, narrow field, maximum burn. It was all automatic. It was all slow motion. It was all high speed. It was all nightmare.

She could see the chopper pilot's head. She could see two of the crew with rifles, sweeping away at the ground below, intent on turning it into an inferno. They had spotted her. The rifles swung towards her. . . .

EDMUND COOPER, a Britisher,
has had his books published
on both sides of the Atlantic.

GENDER GENOCIDE

by Edmund Cooper

ace books

A Division of Charter Communications Inc.
1120 Avenue of the Americas
New York, N.Y. 10036

I

IT WAS a fine summer morning—perfect for Extermination Day. Rura had the gefcar on medium lift, medium cruise, which was about right for the rugged Cumberland Valleys. One hundred and fifty kilometers per hour, one meter above the ground. At that speed, one would be unlikely to encounter any nasty surprises. There was plenty of time to get to the Scottish Highlands and show blood before darkness. In any case, the spotter chopper that circled lazily overhead might report suitable targets long before they got to the Highlands. Some of the regressives were getting bold enough to advance south.

Rura was tired. So, probably, were her companions, Moryn and Olane. The traditional Extermination Eve orgy had been a recordbreaker. No doubt it would go down in College history as one of the great ones of the twenty-fifth century. Rura could remember making love to three girls. After that, things became hazy. Goddess knew how many girls had then made love to her.

Now the gefcar was hissing along the side of Windermere. Sunlight slanted on the fells, translating hills, rocks and moorland into textures of infinite beauty. On such a day as this . . . on such a day as this, thought Rura, what a drag it was to have to hunt down men

5

and daub one's self in their revolting blood. But tradition was tradition. Graduation Day at the College of Exterminators had always involved this symbolic blooding. It was an affirmation of faith, and the end of two years of intensive training.

In two more weeks, thought Rura, *I shall be twenty years old. I shall be entitled to full Womanhood. I shall wear the gold skull and crossbones of a qualified exterminator. Women will desire me. I shall be able to choose.*

Rura felt guilty. She should have been feeling happy. But she felt guilty. Guilty because not happy? Then why not happy? She did not know. She tried to remember the girls she had held and loved. She tried to remember the wide look of surprise in their eyes. She tried to remember lips, breasts, touch, closeness, giving, receiving. But the only thing she could remember was emptiness. Perhaps she had been working too hard.

"Take to the water," said Moryn. "Darling, take to the water. Let's make a valley of foam all along Windermere. Let's make foam in the sunlight. Let's leave a trail behind us to mark Extermination Day."

Rura smiled and swung the ground-effect car onto the lake. It had been such a still lake, like a sheet of glass. But now the blast of air from the gefcar gouged into it, flinging up walls of fine spray through which the sunlight made transient rainbows.

Olane looked back at the dying wake. "We write in water, we write in air," she said strangely. "None of us will ever write in rock."

Olane was one of the girls that Rura had kissed and held and driven to ecstacy on Extermination Eve. She

6

glanced at her, saw the sadness in her eyes, instantly became depressed.

"Olane, darling, we cannot live forever."

"Sometimes," said Olane, "I think we simply cannot live."

Moryn sensed the melancholy and combatted it with instant gaiety. "I have a bottle of brandy with me," she said. "Let us all drink to a fine blooding."

Rura was surprised. "Alcohol is strictly forbidden on Extermination Day. We could be expelled."

"Who would know? There will be blood on our faces, and the brandy bottle will be at the bottom of some Scottish loch. Let us drink and be merry, for today we kill."

Rura spilled her brandy as she pulled away from Windermere and lifted over the mountains. Altogether, there were five gefcars and fifteen novices on the hunt. But no other gefcars were in sight. Only the chopper, circling and hovering like a bird of prey, as indeed it was. Lieutenant Kayt was in the chopper. Rumor had it that she could spot a man at five kilometers.

Olane was hitting the brandy pretty hard. "Darlings, don't think me silly, but I'm afraid of the blooding. I don't know why. I'm just afraid."

Moryn kissed her. "Sweet, there is nothing to be afraid of. I speak truly. There is nothing to be afraid of. The pigs have nothing but swords, knives, spears. Maybe crossbows if they are lucky. We have grenades, we have gas, we have laser guns. So who can harm us?"

"Perhaps we shall harm ourselves."

"Don't be silly. Do you hate men?"

"Of course, I hate men."

"Then there is no problem. Kayt will give us a target. We shall blood ourselves and go home. End of Extermination Day. End of two hard years."

"Two years." Olane sighed. "I never really wanted to be an exterminator. My mother was ambitious for me. It was what she had always wanted."

Moryn raised an eyebrow. "You have a womb mother?"

"Don't be catty," snapped Olane. "You know I was cloned—one of a four-clone. It doesn't make any difference. I still think of Siriol as my mother."

"She is only your clone senior."

"Rot you! She's my mother!"

"Children! Children!" soothed Rura. "Are you going to quarrel, today of all days?"

Moryn poured more brandy. "Darling, I'm sorry. If you want Siriol to be your mother, she *shall* be your mother."

Olane was contrite. "My fault. I shouldn't be so edgy. I'll feel better when this wretched blooding is over."

"I'm going to call Kayt," said Rura. "Find out what's happening." She flicked the transceiver switch and spoke to the chopper.

In the rear seats of the gefcar, Moryn and Olane relaxed, drank brandy, watched the mountains and moors of Cumberland flash by, and looked ahead towards Scotland, impatient to reach the Southern Uplands— the beginning of regressive country. Pig country.

"Kayt says the other four are about ten kilometers ahead of us," said Rura.

"Damn! They will blood before we do!" Moryn looked at the map. "Rura, let's take a shortcut. Ask Kayt for permission to go over the Solway Firth. If we take the sea route, we can save fifty kilometers."

Rura conferred with the chopper. "Permission granted. But Kayt says she must stay with the other four. If there are any targets before we rendezvous in the Southern Uplands, the others will get the benefit."

"Pouff! We'll find our own targets. You can go flat out across Solway and put us half an hour ahead. We'll be blooded before the rest get there. Besides, the sea will be lovely this morning. Have some more brandy."

"No thank you." Rura was emphatic. "I have to pilot this thing. If the blood on our faces turned out to be our own, we should be the laughing stock of London."

Rura swung the gefcar in a tight turn, lifting it over the thousand-meter heights of Skiddaw. It was a clear morning. Fifteen kilometers ahead was the sea, blinding in sunlight, beautiful.

With Skiddaw behind, Rura put her foot down. The gefcar leaped forward. One hundred and eighty kilometers per hour. Two hundred. Two hundred and twenty. Maximum speed, medium high lift. It was wonderful to be racing like this on a column of air to the sea.

It was a golden day. What a pity to spoil it with death, even if only the death of a man.

"Goddess be praised," shouted Moryn, drinking more brandy. "Goddess be praised. We are the elite, the invincibles, the immortals. This day men will die at our hands. I know it. This day we shall remember forever."

The sea was not as flat as Windermere. But it was a gentle sea with the lightest of swells. The gefcar pitched a little, but no one was sick. The sea was gold and blue and hypnotic.

Olane began to cry as the coast of Scotland loomed

ahead. "I don't want to kill anyone," she sobbed. "The day is too lovely for death."

"You will not be killing anyone," said Moryn. "You will only be killing men. A man. A man is nothing. A man is an animal. Do you want an animal to lie on top of you? Do you want it to force your legs open, bite your breasts, fill your womb with the seed of destruction?"

"No! No! No!"

"Then listen to me little one. We shall find our animal. We shall hunt it and kill it. We shall feel its blood upon our faces. And then we shall return to London like conquerors, like true women. We shall be free in our minds and in our hearts. We shall have destroyed the great confidence trick, the million-year degradation."

"I don't want to kill."

"Rest easy. Rura and I will do the killing."

Rura said, "Shall I follow this river, or shall I turn east to rendezvous with the others?"

Moryn looked at the map. "It is only about thirty or forty kilometers out of our way. Follow the river. Men need fresh water, and—for once—we need men."

II

It was pleasant skimming up the river in sunshine with the Scottish hills rearing on either side, thought Rura. It was the sort of day on which one ought to be having a picnic—a lazy picnic on the coast; and afterwards one would swim naked in the sea and then run along the sand and feel salt crystals forming as your flesh dried in the warm air. She sighed. Olane was right. The day was too lovely for death.

The chopper had been out of sight for some time now. It was way over to the east, spotting for the other four gefcars. The odds were that Kayt would find targets for them within the next couple of hours. Then they would blood themselves and turn for home. On the other hand, there was certainly more distinction in finding one's own target. It would be noted in the log. It would be remembered when the question of promotion arose.

Every now and then, Rura called Lieutenant Kayt for a state-of-the-chase report. There had been one sighting: a solitary, kilted male, lucky enough to be near trees. One gefcar had grounded while the three exterminators had hunted him on foot; but he had passed through the wood and taken to the heather. It was almost impossible to find a man lying in the heather on a Scottish hillside. Impossible and dangerous, for you wouldn't see him until you trod on him; and then you would have a dirk in your stomach before you could press a trigger.

Moryn had checked the equipment and was now scanning the sides of the river through binoculars. Olane was still hitting the brandy. Poor Olane! She was right. She never would make an exterminator. She didn't have the temperament. And now she was drinking herself into insensibility; somehow Rura and Moryn would have to cover for her.

"The river leads to Castle Douglas and then to Loch Carlingwark," said Moryn. "We are on a good run, Rura. I smell it."

"What is Castle Douglas?"

"A ghost town. Dead two centuries or more. But there may still be metal in the ruins. The pigs need metal badly. Metal for their dirks and arrowheads, metal for pans for their filthy sows. We shall find targets near Castle Douglas. Bet you twenty Euros."

"How is Olane?"

"Stinking happy. Let her stay that way. She's good in bed, but she doesn't have the stomach for woman's work."

Rura glanced at the pilot's mirror. Olane lay half-sprawled along the rear seat, clutching the brandy bottle. She had unbuttoned her black exterminator shirt and bared her breasts. As the gefcar bounced on wavelets, so her breasts bounced. Last night they had been quite lovely breasts, firm, vibrant, responsive. But now the alcohol had slackened them. They were just lumps of flesh on the body of a girl whose eyes rolled, who was afraid to blood herself on a bright day in summer.

"Take the brandy away from her. Moryn, take it away."

"Screw you, bitch. I heard that," said Olane thickly. "You were cloned from a pig-lover. Your mother grunted while she was being laid."

"Take it away from her!"

"Easy, Rura. Easy. We'll look after her. We'll put the blood on her face while she's sleeping. She won't know a thing."

"I am the pilot of this gefcar. Throw the bottle overboard. That is an order."

A futile order because, as Rura saw, Olane had almost emptied the bottle.

"Sow, bitch!" screamed Olane. "You had me last night. Wasn't I good enough? Weren't my breasts to your liking? Didn't I do the right things with my tongue?"

"Moryn, take it away."

Moryn snatched the bottle. Olane feebly protested, then closed her eyes, sank back and began to snore.

"You were stupid to bring it."

"Darling, how was I to know that Olane was so far gone? Anyway, it will be better for her like this. She won't know a thing."

"You planned it!"

"Of course I planned it," said Moryn. "I love her. Do you hear, I love her! You may have laid her, but I love her."

"All right, Moryn. I receive the message loud and clear. We are still friends?"

"We are still friends."

13

"Then find us a bloody target. The day is going sour."

Moryn took up the glasses once more and searched the banks of the river.

Time passed, the sun beat down. Despite airconditioning, the gefcar was getting stuffy. Rura lowered the windows, letting the warm Scottish breeze and the cold Scottish spray refresh her. Olane groaned in her stupor. Moryn searched the banks with ferocious intensity.

"I can smell the pigs. They are somewhere around—but I can't see them. The trouble is, they can hear us coming."

"I'll cut down to thirty kph.," said Rura. "At that speed, it is barely more than a whisper."

"Blood and afterbirth," said Moryn. "If we don't find something soon, we'll have to go back to the herd."

But even as she spoke, the gefcar swung round a sharp bend in the river; and there was a sudden brief glimpse of movement on the left bank. Movement in the heather.

"Tally ho!" shouted Moryn. "Pigs for the sticking! Ten o'clock high. Put your foot down, baby. Put your foot down. Ten o'clock high and gone to heather. Range fifteen hundred meters."

Rura accelerated and lifted. She swung the gefcar towards the left bank, ten o'clock high. As she turned, she noticed an old bridge half a kilometer upriver. The road to Castle Douglas, no doubt. Moryn had been right. The regressives were stupid to stay near ruined towns; but if they needed metal, what else could they do?

The moorland swept up steeply from the river. Grass gave way to heather, thick Scottish heather. Rura cut

14

in the booster jets, and the gefcar leaped crazily up the rough hillside.

Moryn was arming herself. Laser rifle and grenades. "Five hundred meters . . . one hundred meters . . . lift her, baby. Lift her—now! Circle. We may be lucky enough to see them. They'll move. They won't like the blast from an exterminator car singeing their fat bottoms."

Rura circled and hovered. But, apart from the gefcar's air blast flattening the heather, there was no movement.

"Ground," said Moryn. "Let's get out and burn their balls off."

"How many did you see?"

"Three, I think. Yes, three."

"According to the book, we are not supposed to ground unless we know the exact location."

"Stick the book in your vagina. I know they're here. That's what counts. Goddess damn you, ground, Rura! If you are afraid to do it on foot, you can cover me."

Rura let the gefcar down. It settled at a steep angle, rolling Olane face downwards. She snored and grumbled, but she didn't move.

Moryn leaped out of the car.

"Wait for me," called Rura.

"You're coming, then?"

"Of course I'm coming. Did you think I'd let you take to the heather alone?" Rura lifted her rifle. She didn't like grenades.

For a moment or two the girls stood in the heather, listening. They heard nothing but the whispering of the breeze. It was a lovely breeze, caressing their bodies, stroking their hair with invisible fingers. Rura looked

15

around her. Blue sky, bright sun, hectares of lovely moorland, and a blue-gold thread of river in the valley below. High overhead, a bird hovered. A large bird. Was it an eagle, a hawk? What a wonderful day. Too wonderful for death.

"Come on, Rura. Don't daydream. You'll get an arrow in your breast. Keep about ten meters behind me."

They had moved only a few paces when the first arrow came. It was meant for Moryn. It struck sparks from the barrel shield of her rifle, then whanged off into the heather. It had come from the right, higher on the hillside.

"Tally ho!" said Moryn. "The pigs panic."

She began to climb up the hill. Suddenly, a figure rose from the heather. A kilted, bearded figure, silhouetted against the sky. He had fitted a bolt to his crossbow; but before he could raise it, Moryn used her rifle. There was a burst of smoke and a flash of fire on the man's shoulder. He screamed, dropped the crossbow and fell back to the heather, writhing.

"Tally ho!" Moryn scrambled towards the agitated heather.

He was dirty and sunburned, and his hair was long and his beard was coarse and heavy, and there was pain in his eyes. Pain and hatred.

"Watch for the others, Rura, while I look into this pig's eyes and kill him."

Another figure rose from the heather, fifteen, twenty meters away. It was a boy, a small boy, vainly trying to fit an arrow to his bow.

"Don't!" pleaded the man. "Don't kill."

Moryn snarled, swung her rifle and blasted the boy point-blank. He screamed and fell.

16

"Two down! The day of days. Two down!"

The man at her feet let out a cry of anguish and tried to stand up. Moryn kicked his face. He fell back, groaning.

"My son! My son!"

"Pig, you will live long enough to see us blood ourselves in your son."

Rura cried, "Moryn! Moryn, for the love of goddess, death is enough. Death is enough."

Moryn gave her a strange smile. "The pigs must understand. This is the end of the line. Evolution has finished with them. They are obsolete. Watch this one. I'll get what's left of this spawn. Then we shall blood ourselves at last."

She strode towards the spot where the boy had fallen. But as she moved, another figure rose, not three meters from her. It was a woman, hair long, face distorted, eyes wild. She gave a dreadful cry and rushed at Moryn even as the laser rifle came up.

Moryn must have cut her almost in two, but somehow she kept on coming. She gave a great sigh and fell against Moryn, slithering to the ground.

Moryn staggered a little, turned slowly and looked at Rura. There was an expression of immense frozen surprise in Moryn's eyes. The haft of a dirk protruded from her chest. Her lips moved. The words were barely audible.

"A great blooding," said Moryn. "Look after Olane. I—" She sank to her knees.

"I—I graduate with honor." Then she fell forward, and the dirk was driven through her body.

Rura stood, petrified. Then she rushed to Moryn and turned her over. Her eyes were open, sightless. Blood oozed from her mouth. Rura tried to wipe it away. The blood was warm, so warm. . . .

She was aware of movement, and snatched at the laser rifle. The wounded man was trying to get up. Rura pointed the rifle at him uncertainly.

"May I go to my son? May I put him by my wife?"

At the word *wife*, Rura almost pressed the trigger. It was the dirtiest, the most obscene word in the language. It reeked of possession and slavery and sweaty submission and of the hideous weight of man.

"What can it matter to you where I die?" he asked. His voice was calm, even reasonable. It was not an unpleasant voice. There was no pleading in it, nor was there any anger.

Still Rura did not trust herself to speak.

"Hell, I'm going to him anyway. If you shoot, it doesn't matter. Nothing matters." Painfully, he managed to get to his feet. Blood ran down his arm from the wound at his shoulder. For the first time, Rura smelled the terrible smell of burnt clothing and burnt flesh.

The man's face was gray with pain. He staggered to the boy's body and tried to lift it with his good arm. He couldn't. Unthinking, Rura put the rifle down and went to help.

"Let me," she said, speaking for the first time.

He looked at her amazed.

Rura lifted the child. So thin and light and pale— but with a great hole in his chest. A black, wet hole.

She took the child and laid it by the woman. The woman had fallen on her face. Rura tried to turn her over, but the body was almost severed in half.

The man kneeled down on the heather, touching first the boy's hair, then the woman's, then again the boy's. He had thick, coarse fingers; but they seemed very gentle in their touch.

He knelt on the heather, stroking the boy's hair, not seeing Rura, not seeing anything. "You can kill me, now. Yes, hellbitch, you can kill me now."

Then he pitched forward, unconscious.

III

THERE WAS a medikit in the gefcar. Rura got it and did what she could for the man's shoulder. He had been burned almost to the bone, but only at the tip of the shoulder; so perhaps his muscles would recover.

Rura took the aerosol cylinders one by one. First she sprayed painkiller, then the regenerative jelly, and finally she sprayed a liberal dose of synthaskin. Why was she doing all this for a pig whose sow had just killed Moryn? She did not know. Perhaps it was because sunlight and death were incongruous. She did not know. Anyway, it was not a time for knowing. It was a time for doing.

Moryn had not thrown the brandy bottle overboard. There was still some left. The man was recovering consciousness. She helped him sit up and gave him the brandy. He drank, choked a little, then drank again. Then he flung the empty bottle away into the heather and looked at Rura.

"You are trained to kill, yet you do not. Why is this?"

"I don't know."

"You save me, perhaps, for some private amusement with your friends."

"No. Not that. Presently, I must go—and you must go, if you can. The adjudicators will come to inspect the kills and inquire into the death of my comrade."

He gave her a grim smile. "You have not yet blooded. Yes, I know all about Extermination Day. Whose blood do you choose now—my wife's or my son's?"

"Shut up, pig!" she said fiercely. "Be thankful you are still alive."

He touched the head of his son. "Yes, I have much to be thankful for, have I not? The dead bear witness."

"You held them in thrall," said Rura. "They were your possessions, your slaves."

"You have been well taught. Yes, they were my possessions. *My* wife, *my* son. They loved me."

"You dominated them, you warped their emotions."

"Possibly. I loved them also. I would have died for them, as they died for me. For whom would you die, Madam Exterminator?"

"I may kill you yet," screamed Rura.

"Then you might be doing me a service, dry-womb. For the dead are more precious to me than any living."

Rura picked up her laser rifle. "You are asking for it."

"Yes, clever child, I am asking for it. You are, I suspect, twenty years old. You are not a woman, you are a killing machine. You and your like. You are taking over; and the human race is finished. I do not wish to attend the requiem. I have my own dead to mourn. They, at least, were people."

Rura's finger was on the trigger. "Since history began, men have been the destroyers."

He smiled. "Anything we can do, you can do with less style. You loveless, hygienic killers. Press the trigger, child. Diarmid MacDiarmid will thank you for a quick death."

She put the rifle down. "Diarmid MacDiarmid!"

"No less. Satan, Beelzebub, the great regressive, the violator of women's rights, the pig of pigs, is at your mercy. Shoot and be damned. It will be a graduation to remember."

"Diarmid MacDiarmid!"

"Do me a favor. Tell them I did not weep. Tears are private things. My son and my wife already know that I have wept."

"I heard about you when I was a child," said Rura in amazement. "If I was antisocial, they used to say: 'The Diarmid will get you.'" She smiled. "I used to think of you as some shapeless all-engulfing horror that came in the still of the night."

He also produced the shadow of a smile. "I am not entirely shapeless, I hope; but it is not every man who becomes a legend. Well, are you going to kill the all-engulfing horror, or not?"

"I—I." Rura was confused.

Suddenly he moved. With immense speed and agility, springing like a cat. Rura, off-guard, was knocked down into the heather. And then he was standing over her, the laser rifle held firmly in his one good hand.

"Graduation Day," he said quietly, "is full of surprises. Now we are even, you and I, for I give you back your life."

"What do you want?" Surprisingly, Rura was not afraid. She could not understand why she was not afraid. Moryn was dead, and it had all gone wrong. And she, Rura, had been incredibly stupid.

"What do I want? I want to make a traitor of you,

22

Madam Exterminator. There is honesty for you. Now indulge me in my folly, and tell me your name."

"Rura Alexandra."

"A clone child?"

"Parthenogenetic."

"Ho, ho! One of the so-called naturals. What have they told you about me?"

"That you rape women, that you force them to drink your urine, that you cut off their breasts and kill them."

"All true. All very true." He flung the rifle to her. "I have just raped you, etcetera, etcetera, and now you are a ghost. How do you feel?"

Suddenly, Rura's brain began to work once more. "Listen to me. We have no time for these games. The chopper will want to know why I have not reported. Soon it will be coming to look."

"You have your toy," he said. "You, too, can graduate with honor."

"I don't want to kill you," she cried desperately.

"Ah, so? An exterminator who does not wish to kill. A traitor, indeed."

"You must get away from here."

"Perhaps I do not wish to get away from here."

"You must! You must!"

He sighed. "We are losing the war, Rura Alexandra. A good general prefers to die on the battlefield. I am not a good general; but I am sentimental. I wish to remain awhile with my dead."

"There isn't time. The chopper will investigate."

"For me there is time. A little. You see, I discovered something this morning. I discovered it when your late lethal friend destroyed those I love. I am no longer afraid to die. It is a fine feeling. . . . You are the one

23

who must get away. I can afford to remain. But before you go, share something with me. Look at the faces of my dead."

Gently, he turned the woman so that her sightless eyes were towards the sky. Her face was thin, lined, sunburned. Her lips were full. There were white streaks in her hair. She looked old.

"Flora MacDiarmid, age thirty-two, child of the heather. She gave me two sons. One died of hunger, too young even to know this world. One died of—well, Rura Alexandra, what did my other son die of?"

He kissed the lips of the dead woman and closed her eyes. Then he turned to the child. "Ewan MacDiarmid, age ten, child of the heather, child of hunger, child of fear. He had the misfortune to be born of love and to be sustained by love in a world poisoned by hate. Look at his face, Madam Exterminator. Be proud that your comrade saved you from rape and sadism at his hands."

Rura looked at the child, pale, peaceful. There was no sign of the beast on him. He looked as if he had been a very gentle child.

Tears welled silently in her eyes and ran down her face.

"Well, indeed," said Diarmid. "I have lived to see a miracle, and my time is spent. I have lived to see an exterminator weep for a boy child."

"Shut up, damn you! I must think. I must think. We are running out of time. One of my crew is dead, the other is drunk in the gefcar, there are two dead regressives in the heather—and you are still alive."

He gestured towards the rifle. "The last problem is easily solved. Then you can call your commander, tell her of the terrible battle that took place, blood yourself, get witnesses for the body count and collect your citation. There is a great future ahead of you, Rura Alexandra."

"Do you really want to die?"

"Let us say that I am tired of living. The race goes not to the swift, nor the battle to the strong."

"What does that mean?"

"Only that I am tired."

"Then live with your fatigue. Have you ever ridden in a gefcar?"

"No."

"I will take you away from here, then I will come back and arrange matters."

He smiled. "Have you ever been kissed by a man?"

"No!" The thought was revolting.

Ignoring the rifle, he held her. "Then I will kiss you, and if you do not kill me, I will ride in your gefcar."

He kissed her on the lips. She struggled, but with one arm he managed to hold her. The rifle dropped. There was something terrible about the kiss. It was like no other kiss she had ever known. It was humiliating, it was degrading, it was disturbing. It drained strength from her limbs, filled her head with nightmares.

He let her go.

"Well, exterminator. That was a kind of rape, was it not? Incidentally, you dropped your rifle."

"Yes," was all she could say. "Yes, I dropped the rifle." She picked it up.

"And now, if you do not kill me, I will ride in your gefcar. Where shall we go?"

"Castle Douglas, perhaps?"

. "Oddly, Castle Douglas is safe for me. There are many ruins, you see. The ruins give cover. Saving your presence, exterminators do not care for individual combat; and that is what cover involves."

"You will have to travel with Olane, who is drunk. Do not touch her. Do not let her see you."

He gave a bitter laugh. "Already we are conspirators."

She took him to Castle Douglas. As the gefcar began to move, Olane grumbled sleepily. After a time she gave a strange grunt, then became silent. It was only a few minutes' lift along the river. Kayt called twice and was ignored. Rura jumped the bridge on boost, then lifted to high boost and rode over rubble and masonry to what was left of the town square. She cut the motors. There was nothing but a windswept silence.

She got out of the gefcar. Diarmid MacDiarmid followed her.

"Don't stay long," he warned. "Some of my friends are quite handy with the crossbow."

"How do you know they are here?"

"I don't. I suspect. I always suspect."

Sunlight made the ruined town seem very desolate. Here and there birds squabbled, rising noisily into the blue.

"I have left you a souvenir in your gefcar," said Diarmid MacDiarmid. "I shall walk away slowly. I shall give you time to decide whether to shoot. But I thank you for courtesies. For Flora and Ewan, I thank you for courtesies."

"Live long," called Rura, not knowing what she was saying. "Live long. Teach us to be women."

Then she went back to the gefcar and found Olane with a dirk through her breast. She lifted the laser rifle and centered on the spine of Diarmid MacDiarmid. But she could not press the trigger.

Birds flapped noisily overhead, and she tried to decide what to do.

IV

SOMETHING HAD gone wrong inside Rura's mind. She knew that. Some dark, psychotic demon was running amok. All her training counted for nothing. She was filled with misery and fear and a dreadful compulsion to conceal the obscene truth.

She wasn't thinking any more—thought was too painful. She was simply following the demon, who had promised her that the events of the morning could be erased as if they had not happened.

Somehow, she got the gefcar back to that terrible hillside. Somehow, she carried poor, timid Olane—who had died as Moryn had died—to lie with the woman who loved her. In death they looked so small, almost as small and pale as Ewan MacDiarmid, the boy child.

Olane's breasts, bloody and slack, were bared to the wind and the sky. Rura had been afraid to take out the dirk. Oddly, it lay deep in Olane in almost the identical spot that Flora MacDiarmid's dirk had struck Moryn. Oddly, as they lay there, Olane and Moryn looked like lovers who had found release from some secret anguish in a shared death. Perhaps that was not too far from the truth.

Rura placed Moryn's arm, stiffening a little, protectively round Olane's shoulder. She looked on them for the last time.

Then the demon told her what to do.

A light breeze was blowing steadily up the hillside. Rura went down a few meters below where she had parked the gefcar. She set her laser rifle at maximum power, depressed the trigger and swung the rifle round in a wide sweep, firing the heather. It was green but there had been no rain for days; the breeze was right and it burned well. Obviously, the demon knew about such things.

A line of flame and smoke swept upwards. The smoke would be visible to an alert chopper crew forty or fifty kilometers away.

Rura sat down in the heather, below the fireline, resting her face in her hands, her elbows on her knees, wondering what had happened to her, wondering about the identity and purpose of the demon inside her. She did not move even when the gefcar went up with a great bang and in a great gout of flame.

She did not move when the chopper came and circled. She did not move when it touched down and Lieutenant Kayt came towards her. She should have jumped smartly to attention; but she just sat there.

Kayt was saying something. Kayt was always saying something. She was a big woman, and she liked to lay novices. She had laid Rura once, but that was in another country; and besides, the wench was dead.

Kayt was gentle. She went on talking. She soothed and reassured. And presently the demon gave Rura the right words.

"There were about eight of them, I think. But we didn't know that at first. We only saw two. We circled and searched, regulation procedure. Then I grounded and covered Moryn as she went to take out a bearded male with a crossbow. He tried to shoot, but she caught him in the shoulder. Then they were coming up at us out of the heather. One had a laser weapon. I tried to take him out; but there wre others, closer. I didn't see what happened to Olane. She was covering me. When I heard her scream, I tried to help her. But she died. And then there was nothing but the heather burning. I—I carried Olane . . . I carried Olane, and then I saw what had happened to Moryn . . . and the heather was burning, and the pigs had gone. And there was nothing, no one."

"Not all the pigs had gone," said Kayt. "We found two —and there is blood on your face."

"Blood on my face?' Whose blood? Olane's. Most certainly Olane's.

"It is my considered opinion," said Kayt, stroking her hair, "that you have graduated with honor. That is how my report will read. When you have recovered, we will assemble the facts together carefully. There will be an inquiry, of course. But there is blood on your face, and two regressives are dead. Do you understand, Rura? Two are dead. One for Moryn. One for Olane. You graduate with honor."

There was a court of inquiry. Quite composed, Rura and the demon attended it. The demon's story was more coherent this time. The loose ends were tied up.

Rura was triumphantly acquitted of the formal charges of cowardice and negligence. She graduated as an Exterminator, First Class, and was awarded the silver nipple for gallantry.

Lieutenant Kayt become her lover.

V

LIBERATION HOUSE, formerly Buckingham Palace, was connected by a broad and splendid tree-lined avenue to Emancipation Square, formerly Trafalgar Square, and the semi-sacred shrine of Germaine's Needle, formerly Nelson's Column. Liberation House was the residence of the College of Exterminators. It was also the destination of every energetic, red-blooded, ambitious girl with an aggression quotient of one hundred and twenty plus in the Republic of Anglia.

Admission to the College of Exterminators was by State Scholarship, patronessage, and open competition. Every two years one thousand eager novices—the cream of the Republic's womanhood—came to Liberation House to endure the discipline and acquire the skills that would eventually lead to the gold skull and crossbones. Every two years, about eight hundred qualified exterminators —on average, one in five had fallen by the wayside —said hail and farewell to the novices on Last and First Day.

There were speeches, celebrations, wakes, raggings. The tradition had been established for the best part of a century.

Rura was happy and sad. It was ten days since graduation, since the deaths of Olane and Moryn; and now here was Last and First Day, the end of novitiate, the beginning of a career.

It was a wet morning. Rain trickled dully down the window of her cell. She lay in her rumpled bed while Lieutenant Kayt kissed her and stroked her and whispered things of great tenderness, planning for the future.

Rura was aware of Kayt's hands upon her body, but felt nothing. Kayt was a sweet and truly aggressive woman. But there was something lacking. She did not have the touch of fire. So the love affair was doomed, even if Kayt did not already know it.

Why did Rura feel nothing? Was it because of Olane, who died drunk, unknowing? Was it because of Moryn, whose death was both absurd and heroic? Was it because of a dirty, bearded male who stroked a boy child's hair, and did not care whether he lived or died?

Rura was too confused, too empty, to be able to think coherently. She tried to respond to Kayt's caresses; but there was no magic singing in her blood. No love, no ecstasy. Nothing.

"What is it darling?" asked Kayt, trying to contain her exasperation. "You got a First Class and the silver nipple. I fixed it. What's wrong?"

Rura kissed her and held her close. "I don't know, sweet amazon. I simply don't know. Perhaps I'm tired. It's a hard course. Perhaps now that it is all over, the tiredness is hitting me."

"A holiday, that's it," said Kayt, stroking her hair. "You will have a week before you take up your posting. I can apply for special leave—the damned novices are never fit for anything in the first week—and we'll go away together to some quiet place where—"

"No, please."

"You don't want to go away with me?"

"It's not that. Honestly, it's not that."

"Well, what is it then?"

"I told you. I just don't know."

Kayt sighed. "Oh, well, I can wait. I suppose I can wait. I know we are right for each other. I fixed it for you, Rura. Remember that. I fixed it. I don't know quite what happened up there in the heather, and you don't ever have to tell me. But I do know it wasn't what was in my report."

"I'm sorry. I really am sorry."

Lieutenant Kayt got out of bed and looked at her watch. "It is two and a half hours to Last and First Day Address. By that time, your bags have to be packed, the cell has to be clean, the novice has to be introduced, and you have to be in dress uniform. Baby, we'd better pull the plug out."

Rura sighed and got out of bed. She would have much preferred to pull the sheets over her head, close her eyes and sink into a state of nothingness.

Kayt held her close, breasts to breasts, belly to belly, lips to lips.

"You do love me, Rura?"

"Yes, I—I do love you."

"That's all right then. We'll work something out. Now let's get something to eat. You have never had to sit through one of Curie Milford's Last and First Day speeches before. I have. You need a full stomach. Then, with a bit of luck, you can doze."

Rura looked through the window. The rain was coming down steadily, the sky was an even gray. She thought of all the anxious and nervous novices making their way to Liberation House. She thought of herself, just as anxious and nervous, two years ago. Then, Graduation Day and Last and First Day had seemed the two most important events that would ever happen in the world.

And now she felt nothing. And the rain was coming down. And when she looked through the window and gazed along the Mall, she could see nothing but ghosts and burning heather.

And the man she had not had the courage to kill.

VI

Since the expansion of the College of Exterminators in the early decades of the twenty-thirs century, Liberation House had not possessed a hall big enough to contain the three thousand women—guests, graduates, novices and staff—who attended the ceremonies of Last and First Day. The hail and farewell service was therefore carried out in the Hall of Light, a great dome of hiduminium and milky glass that was the last major work of the architect Cleo Castle before she was blinded by a pig while hunting in the Welsh hills.

Traditionally the Last and First Day speech was made by the prime minister. Madam Curie Milford had broken all records since the Dark Ages by being the first prime minister of the Republic of Anglia to hold office continuously for more than twelve years. This was her sixth official attendance at the Hall of Light.

As a recently graduated Exterminator First Class, Rura, with her cell novice sitting on her right, had a seat only four rows from the stage. Directly in front of her on the stage was the lectern where Curie Milford now stood. Behind the prime minister sat a row of dignitaries and the principal of the college. Behind them, on several rising tiers, sat the rest of the college staff, including Lieutenant Kayt.

Kayt caught Rura's eye and smiled. Rura tried to smile back; but her face felt frozen. She was immensely conscious of the girl in the white tunic by her side, Jolan Knight, age eighteen.

Rura had been introduced to Jolan only an hour before the ceremony, when she had formally handed over the key to her cell. Jolan had gazed at the black tunic, the First Class chevron, the silver nipple and the gold skull and crossbones with awe verging upon adoration. She realized, she said, that she was taking over the cell of an outstanding graduate. She hoped she would be worthy. In a not very subtle way, she tried to offer herself. Perhaps it would have increased her confidence if she could have been embraced by a graduate who had gained the silver nipple for gallantry. Or perhaps she just wanted to boast. She was a pretty little thing, full of guile and innocence and enthusiasm. Rura felt tremendously sorry for her. It was one thing to absorb extermination theory. It was another thing to come face-to-face with a regressive in the heather. She wondered what the adoring Jolan would think if she knew that this graduate with the silver nipple had chosen not to exterminate Diarmid MacDiarmid. . . .

The hymn, *O Goddess, our help in ages past,* had ended. Silence had fallen in the Hall of Light. It was time for Curie Milford to speak.

She was a tall woman, surprisingly tall, nearly two meters; but beautifully proportioned. And she carried her age well. She must be seventy years old, but she had long golden hair, bright blue eyes, and the face of a woman who could be serene, or passionate, or dominant, at will. Truly, she was hypnotic. It was rumored that three of her lovers had suicided when she had dismissed them.

"Sisters, women, Exterminators," began Curie Milford, "this is as proud a day for me as it is for you who wear the skull and crossbones after two years of dedication, after two years of hard discipline and intensive training. It is a proud day for me because it is the sixth time I have been privileged to speak in the Hall of Light—a record in our political history, as I am sure you know. It may well be—the vagaries of politics being as uncertain as the vagaries of horse-racing—that this will be the last time."

Polite, sceptical laughter, and a few cries of: "Stay with us, Curie."

"So," continued the prime minister, sweeping back the golden hair and thus subtly calling attention to its length and youthfulness, "I desire to speak to you as if it were the last time. If I am not returned at the forthcoming election, I shall at least have had the satisfaction of knowing that I have said to you exterminators, upon whom the peace of the realm depends utterly, exactly what I wanted to say.

"It is more than two and a half centuries now since we threw off the yoke of slavery, since we expelled the last men, the last troublemakers, from this civilized society of the Republic of Anglia. They thought they were indispensable. They thought that womankind could not get along without them. History shows how wrong they were. How very wrong they were."

Applause, laughter, cheers.

"In two hundred and fifty years," went on Curie Milford, deriving strength from audience response, "there have been no major wars throughout the world. We have entered the golden age of human history. Why is this? Of course, you know the answer. It is because our sisters in Europe and Asia and America profited by our example. They also threw off the yoke of slavery. They also drove out the men."

More applause. Longer applause. The prime minister did not attemp to stop it. She was content to let it roll and wait until it had abated.

"However, may I be heretical for a moment? May I forget my high office and speak as a woman?"

Cries of: "Yes! Yes. Tell us Curie. Tell us what you want."

"Then I will be honest. I think our ancestresses, those courageous women who laid the foundations of freedom, betrayed themselves. And, therefore, ultimately they betrayed us. They betrayed themselves, my sisters, because of their own weakness. They should not have driven the men out."

The audience remained silent.

"I repeat: they should not have driven the remaining men out. It was a great mistake. It has cost us a great deal. It has caused us to raise an elite of women who are prepared to hazard themselves, to accept unthinkable risks, for the safety of the state. No, my friends and sisters, our revered ancestresses should not have driven the men out. They should have exterminated them one and all."

Hysterical applause. The prime minister enjoyed being unable to continue for some time. But at last she was allowed to continue.

"We, here today, are all witnesses to that mistake.

The regressives in the Scottish Highlands—there are few, I am glad to say, now left in Wales—are desperately trying to increase their numbers. Occasionally, they manage to raid our more exposed villages, our seminaries and schools. They need women badly, and I do not have to tell you the abominable purpose for which the women are needed. The question is: why do these regressives want to increase their numbers? There is only one answer. They cannot accept their defeat as permanent. They are foolish enough to look forward to a time when man can once more be the master, and woman will once more be reduced to the sex object, the breeding machine, the creature of bondage. Shall we permit the Dark Ages ever to return?"

Cries of: "No! No! Never again. The pigs must die."

"Yes," went on Curie Milford, "the message is clear. The pigs must die. Nature, evolution, gave them their chance. They failed to meet the challenge. They used women as animals. They produced civilizations that flourished by the sword and perished by the sword. Their creed was violence, their strength was based on slavery. But in the end, they only succeeded in turning their biological weapons upon themselves. It was men who resorted to microbiological warfare. It was men who, as an act of desperation, unleashed the Black Death in the middle of the twenty-first century. Perhaps it was poetic justice that the Black Death destroyed more male children than female children. Or perhaps there is another explanation. Could it be, my sisters, that we were stronger than they? Could it be that we were more fitted for survival?"

In the Hall of Light, women began to clap their

hands, stamp their feet, shout. "We were stronger! We *are* stronger! The pigs are weak! We are the inheritors! No more men! No more men! No more men!"

Curie Milford let the chant grow in violence until it seemed as if the great dome must be shattered by the violence of sound. Then she held up her hand, and there was silence.

"Their popes told them to abuse our bodies to breed cannon fodder," she said.

"Yes, yes!" came the response. "Damn the popes! Damn the priests! Damn the male godhead!"

"Their dictators told them to manufacture guns and bombs to destroy women and children."

"Yes, yes! Napoleon, Hitler, Stalin, Mao Tse Tung—all men."

"Their writers portrayed women as weak, irresponsible, inferior."

"Yes, yes! Lawrence, Zola, Tolstoy—all deceivers."

"Do we want to see their like again?"

"No, never! Kill the pigs! Never let them rise again. Never!"

The prime minister, relaxed, waited for the turmoil and the hysteria to die down.

"Never let them rise again," she echoed. "That is what I believe, my sisters. I believe it passionately. I believe it with all my heart. That is why this Last and First Day is for me a very special day. On this island of ours, the number of regressives is falling slowly but steadily. And the number of trained exterminators—as we see by today's splendid ranks of the gold skull and crossbones—is increasing.

"The College of Exterminators is a great institution. But I tell you now, and I tell you frankly, I look forward to the time when the disciplines of Liberation House are no longer concerned with death but only with liberation. We can achieve it, my friends and sisters. We can achieve it soon. I believe that, given the will, the generation of novices we see here—the dedicated girls we see before us in their white tunics—and the black rows of newly qualified exterminators will be the last needed to clear this island of vermin. Thereafter, I believe, there will be no need to defend ourselves from the dangerous animal called man. Because man will have ceased to exist. To this end, I pledge my administration. To this end, all here are dedicated. Who, then, can stand against us?"

The cheering lasted for more than five minutes.

The girl by the side of Rura was laughing and crying and shouting. "Isn't she wonderful? Isn't Curie Milford terrific?"

"Yes," said Rura dully. "She's out of this world."

And thought of Olane, who did not want to kill; and of Diarmid MacDiarmid, who did not want to live.

VII

Rura was assigned to the third company of the Border Regiment, the headquarters of which was in Carlisle, north of the Lake District, south of the Solway Firth. Before reporting for duty, she had almost a week to kill. She didn't want to spend it with Kayt—well, not all of it. She didn't want to spend it with anyone.

Which was odd.

Graduation should be a time for celebrating. Graduation and one's twentieth birthday. A time for parties and friends. A time for excitement and anticipation. *I am truly a woman now*, thought Rura. *I am entitled both to kill and to vote. It ought to mean a great deal.* It didn't seem to mean anything.

There was a time when the idea of killing men had seemed romantic, pleasurable. But Rura had been present at the deaths of four people; and the smell of burning flesh was still in her nostrils. And nightmares came to her. And questions rose in her mind—questions that were heretical, obscene, unanswerable. . . .

Traditionally, on the night of Last and First Day, Liberation House was the scene of one super-colossal party where novices, graduates and staff forgot their rank and treated each other as joyful, sensuous, responsive women. Traditionally, the Day-Night Dance cel-ebrated ends and beginnings without regard for rank or protocol. For the graduates there was much to rem-ember; for the novices there was much to learn. How better than to combine the operations in each other's arms to the strains of the waltz or the strains of an ecstatic bed?

Rura presented herself dutifully and danced twice with Kayt and twice with Jolan. She must have been in a totally passive mood because both Kayt and Jolan assumed the role of aggressor. They danced with her, they kissed her and fondled her. And it all meant nothing. She managed to slip away long before midnight.

She took her bags to the Pankhurst Hotel in Park Lane, got a room, ordered a bottle of whiskey and sat on the bed drinking herself into a mindless stupor.

There were private toasts.

"To Moryn. Without fear, without reason. Rest well, Moryn. You graduated with honor."

Down went a generous dose of neat whiskey.

"To lovely Olane, who did not know, and who will never know."

Another generous dose.

"To Flora MacDiarmid, slave of man, sleep well now in liberation."

The whiskey went down easily. But Rura could still see the lined face, the white hair.

"To Ewan MacDiarmid, son of man, who died before he had lived."

Rura shivered. The whiskey tasted bitter.

"To Diarmid MacDiarmid," she cried. "Pig, destroyer, slave-owner. Damn you in hell!"

She drank the whiskey in a gulp. Then she fell back

on the bed and let the tears come. Whiskey tears. They meant nothing. Only that Rura Alexandra, Exterminator First Class, was drunk and stupid. Stupid and drunk.

The room began to spin; and there was nothing but a dulled anguish until morning.

Rura woke early. Her hands were shaking. All of her was shaking. She went into the bathroom, took off her clothes and stood under the shower. She could have had a hot shower, a warm shower, a tepid shower. She chose to take it ice-cold as a form of punishment. She stood there until she shivered, until her whole body seemed to have become numb. Then she turned off the shower, dried herself and dressed.

It was barely daybreak. She crept out of the quiet hotel and went for a walk in Hyde Park. The air smelled wonderful and clean. There was dew on the grass.

She walked in the park, enjoying the quiet intimacy of early morning. *This is a time*, she thought, *when you can be truly alone; and yet you are not alone, you are part of everything—the grass, the trees, the sky*. She went to the Serpentine, and stood staring at the still sheet of water. There was not a breath of wind, and the Serpentine was clear as a mirror. Rura looked at the reflections of trees, marveling at the drowned upside-down world; the marvelous symmetry of object and image. She was trying very hard not to think; and for a time she succeeded.

Presently she stood right at the water's edge and looked down at her own face. It seemed blank. Was it really the face of a dedicated exterminator? Was it the face of one who belonged—as Curie Milford had prophesied—to the generation that would eliminate men forever?

Suddenly, another face appeared beside hers.

"Give me a Euro for breakfast, dear, and good luck to you. The party is over; but the silver nipple says that you blooded well. There will be honorable stains on that crisp uniform before the year ends."

Rura turned to look at the woman who had invaded her privacy. A tramp. An old, beaten woman, possibly sixty. She was dressed in shapeless, tattered things. She carried a battered hold-all. An exterminator's hold-all. The skull and crossbones were emblazoned on the black leather. It was illegal for a civilian to use exterminator equipment.

"Where did you get that?"

The woman laughed, running a hand through her wispy gray hair. "Don't run me in, dear. You won't win. I used to be a captain in the Welsh Guard. Upon retirement, commissioned officers are entitled to retain insignia and accouterments—unless dishonorably discharged."

"You were not dishonorably discharged?"

"I resigned my commission."

"Why?"

"I was pregnant, dear. You must have heard the word. Pregnant. I'd been had by a man."

Rura wanted to be sick. Last night's whiskey seemed to be coming back into her throat. But curiosity triumphed over nausea.

"What do you mean—you'd been had by a man?"

"Just that. It was twenty years ago—about the time you were being cloned, I'd say."

"I'm parthenogenetic."

"Ah, the elite! Congratulations. Well, are you going to give me a Euro for breakfast?"

Rura knew she would give her some money, anyway.

But she pretended to be indecisive. "I might. Tell me more."

"It's the story of my life you want? That costs more than a Euro."

"It is not the story of your life I want, and I have more than a Euro."

The old woman laughed. "How predictable. Just the fascinating, gory details. Well, Madam Exterminator, make me an offer."

Rura felt sick. Sick and dirty. But she wanted to know. She made an effort to control her reactions. "If the story is both good and true," she said evenly, "I will give you five Euros."

"Make it ten. It's worth it—to both of us."

"I will decide."

"Fair enough. Being newly graduated and wet behind the ears, you are doubtless a woman of honor. Do you have any pot?"

"Goddess rot you, you know I wouldn't have any pot."

"Oh, well. You'll learn. . . . It was, as I say, twenty years ago. There were lots of pigs in Wales, then. Enough to keep us happy and gainfully occupied. . . . Have you ever been to Caernarvon? It's a dead city, of course. Used to have some religious or monarchical significance, I'm told. Before the Dark Ages, I think."

"No, I haven't been to Caernarvon."

"No matter. I was stationed there. Quite a hot spot in my time. You see, Wales was crawling with pigs. We had a ball . . . yes, we had quite a ball. We'd take the gefcars out at daybreak, and you could practically guarantee half a dozen bloodings before lunch. Then we'd frolic for the rest of the day, then go back to base, enter the kills and make love. Halcyon days. We shall not see their like again." The old woman looked across the Serpentine, seeing nothing, smiling to herself.

"Get to the point. You're losing money rapidly."

"Oh yes, where was I? Caernarvon. . . . It was a June morning. A marvelous June morning. Classic summer. . . . We were keen in those days. Got moving before it was light. Thought we might spot one of their fires, you see. I'd planned a pretty route, round the foothills of Snowdon, then down the Lleyn Peninsula and across the sea to South Wales and the Milford Haven area. There were supposed to be several tribes of pigs around Milford Haven—they could still scavenge oil from the derelict refineries—and, anyway, there was a chance we might surprise one or two fishing boats on the way. They had to fish. Couldn't get enough food from the land. Yes, it was a fine morning, the sea like glass. . . ." She sighed.

"Get on with it," snapped Rura.

"In a hurry for the sex, are you?"

Rura turned away.

"No, wait. It happened after lunch. We'd sighted a fishing boat on the way down—there were two pigs in it, I think—and burned it out of the water. So there was no real need for further scalps. But my crew were both young and just out of college; and there it is. We'd parked on a lovely hillside, and it was a warm day, and I wanted to sunbathe, and they wanted to be off spilling more blood. In the end I let them take the gefcar, while I stayed and sunned myself, with a laser rifle handy, just in case." She laughed. "Trouble is, we'd had a glass of wine, and it was such a warm afternoon, and I just fell asleep. Captains of the Welsh Guard should not fall asleep on a hillside in pig country on a sunny afternoon. The next thing I knew, I'd been hit on the head and kicked in the stomach—not hard enough for serious injury, but hard enough to take the fight out of me. By the time I could focus, I was staring down the barrel of my own laser rifle. . . . He was a big man, big but thin with hunger. Big and sunburned, and with bright red hair and a red beard." She laughed. "He looked like one of the pirates I used to read about as a child, before such innocent books were put on the Index."

"Was he—was he alone?" asked Rura.

"He was alone. At least, I didn't see any more. He said very quietly, 'Hellbitch, you've run out of luck.' I thought he was going to kill me. I forget what I said, but it was just something stupid to let him see I wasn't going to squeal. He just grinned and said, 'Take your uniform off, exterminator, before I burn it on your body.' I didn't move, so he put the rifle on minimum burn, and began to slow-roast me. . . . I can tell you, chicken, I was out of that uniform in ten seconds flat. And there was I, naked, on this Welsh hillside with this great red-haired animal laughing fit to bust. Then he put the rifle down very leisurely and said, 'They made an exterminator of you. Now I'll make a woman of you.' This was my chance, I thought. I gave him a flying drop-kick. We both went down. But before I could get up, he was on top of me. I struggled, of course. He hit me a couple of times— again, not enough to really hurt, but enough to let me know that his strength was much greater than mine. . . . Do you know anything about rape, chicken?"

Rura shuddered. "Of course I know about rape."

The woman laughed dreadfully, displaying broken yellow teeth. "Well, I can now reveal to you that it's a myth, chicken, a myth. No woman—particularly an exterminator—who is conscious and uninjured can be raped. So I'll tell you what happened, sweet. I got tired of being punched, and I got tired of struggling uselessly. And the revulsion and the feeling of sickness just sort of died. And the weight on top of me seemed to be—well, interesting. And when he pinioned my arms and bit my throat and dug his fingers into my breast, it all hurt like hell. But, chicken, it aroused me. Goddess, how it aroused me. So I let him enter. And he grunted and I groaned, and we thrashed about like a couple of mindless creatures in frenzy. I tell you, I never knew what a climax was until that red-haired animal squirted his semen into my womb."

Rura swayed. She felt she was going to faint. She felt she was going to be sick. But, dammit, she would do neither. She would not give this wretched woman the satisfaction of knowing what a dreadful effect she was having.

"What's the matter, chicken? You look pale. Are you all right?"

"Of course I'm all right."

"Never mind. You're through the worst. I was too far gone to hear the gefcar. But Redbeard heard it. He whipped out of me, scrambled to his feet and tried to run down the hillside while fastening up his trews. I came out of the trance and pulled myself together just in time to see one of my jolly little crew burn the back of his head off. I don't remember much more. They kept me sedated for a few days. The real trouble started when I found I was pregnant. Abortion, of course. No problem. But the big joke, chicken, was that I didn't want to abort. So I resigned my commission and took the first job I could get—laboring in a ponics farm. However, there was more fun to follow. I miscarried in the fifth month. Boy child, of course. How's that?"

Rura didn't answer, didn't trust herself to speak.

Again the woman laughed. "I've been moving around ever since. Can't seem to settle to anything. I don't know, maybe I'm still looking for a replay with a non-existent red-haired pirate. Don't you think that's funny?"

Rura couldn't face her. She turned away and looked at the Serpentine, at the clean, clean water.

"Yes, it's very funny."

"I told you it was worth ten Euros."

Mechanically, Rura felt for her wallet. She simply could not bear to look at the woman any more. "Here. Take—take what you need."

"Thanks. You're well-upholstered, chicken, so I have taken three fives. All right?"

"All right." She felt the coarse fingers as the woman gave her back the wallet; but she didn't turn round.

"Good hunting, Madam Exterminator."

"Good . . . good—" Rura couldn't finish. She could think of nothing reasonable to say that began with the word good. She could think of nothing at all to say. Her mind was numb.

She heard the footsteps fade away. She just stood there by the Serpentine, gazing at the water, silently and frantically telling herself how clean it looked. She stood there a long time, until the sun was quite high above the horizon.

VIII

RURA MANAGED to have a couple of days to herself before Kayt found her. During that time she did nothing but walk aimlessly around London, drink and think. Or try not to think.

On the morning of her encounter with the ex-captain of the Welsh Guard, she went back to the Pankhurst Hotel and somehow managed to eat breakfast. The food was good food; but it tasted of nothing. It was just something to occupy her. Eating was just something to do. She sat at a table by herself, watched the other guests, and tried to behave normally. Two or three girls, obviously in love with uniforms, tried to attract her attention, smiling invitingly whenever they thought she was looking their way. A strikingly beautiful woman with pure white hair came across to her table and asked if she were lonely. The woman wore a large diamond ring and well-cut clothes, and looked far too prosperous to be a hotel prostitute. Rura said that she expected to be joined presently. The woman gave her a sweet smile and went away.

After breakfast, Rura went up to her room. The chambermaid had left everything neat and tidy, and the room was anonymous once more. Rura looked at herself in the mirror. Long but not unattractive face. Straight brown hair, the short regulation length. Dark patches under the eyes. High cheekbones. Full lips. No expression at all. The face of a stranger. A disturbing stranger.

She wanted to get away from this odd person who stared blankly at her. She got out of the hotel and started walking. She found herself in Piccadilly Circus. There was a statue in Piccadilly Circus. Once, long ago, it had been Eros. Now it was Aphrodite.

Was it truly only women who could love? Were men nothing but destroyers? Everyone knew, of course, that Shakespeare and Leonardo were women in disguise. Women competing in a man's world. But there must have been great men who did not destroy. Men who could love. . . .

Why must there have been men who could love? Human history—*men's* history—was one long bloody record of anguish. Until women had cried enough. Until the women had driven out the men and brought in sanity. Stable government, sensible economics, no more wars.

And yet, to exterminate is to destroy. I am an exterminator, therefore I am a destroyer. But what must I destroy? Only the seeds of destruction itself. Only men.

Later, she found herself walking along the Embankment, looking up at what was once Queen's College, now the College of Inseminators.

I should have been an inseminator, Rura told herself. *I should have been more concerned with creating life than with destroying it.*

Waterloo Bridge was being demolished. Many of the bridges across the Thames were being demolished. Who needs bridges when gefcars will whisper sweetly over the water? Let the Thames run free.

Waterloo. A battle. An orgy of destruction conceived and executed by men. And how could one rate such a battle, such a victory, against the labor pains of all the women who had borne all the soldiers whose blood was shed?

Curie Milford is right, thought Rura. *Everyone is right. I am right. There will be no lasting peace until the last man is exterminated.*

But what of the captain of the Welsh Guard who had met her Waterloo on a sunny hillside long ago?

"She enjoyed it!" cried Rura in horror. "She enjoyed it!"

Passers-by stared at her. She did not notice.

A dirty, sweaty man reducing a trained and intelligent woman to a heap of palpitating flesh. It was disgusting, it was degrading, it was unthinkable.

"She lost the baby! She should have killed the brat! She should have killed it!"

And yet the ex-captain of the Welsh Guard had spent twenty years in mourning. Twenty years and the destruction of a career because a man had forced his flesh into hers.

Rura walked on, mindless, unseeing. Brawny laborers, with breasts like wedges of granite, were building a thirty-story block to house a new government department. They whistled at her; but she didn't hear.

Presently, she found a bar and began to drink. Presently, she discovered to her amazement that the sun had gone and the stars were out. She could still stand. She could still walk, after a fashion. She found a gef-taxi and carefully explained that she wished to be deposited at the Pankhurst Hotel.

When she got back, the beautiful woman with the

white hair was lying in her bed. Rura did not complain. She was beyond complaint. She just took off her clothes and fell into bed, and let the white-haired woman do what she wished.

. In the morning the woman departed, leaving one hundred Euros behind. Rura—head aching abominably—managed to laugh. Who pays whom for what?

She showered and went down to breakfast. The white-haired woman was nowhere to be seen. Was she cultivating another victim? And did it matter?

Rura went walking again. And drinking. When she eventually got back to her hotel, Lieutenant Kayt was in her room.

Déjà vu. Rura wanted to laugh. She laughed.

"What the hell is this all about?" demanded Kayt. "I've been looking for you everywhere. What are you trying to do?"

"Nothing. I've not been doing anything."

"Rura, something's happened to you. Those damn pigs. You need looking after. Otherwise you'll go to pieces. I love you, Rura. I love you."

"I love you, too."

"Then, for Goddess' sake, we've got something to celebrate. I'm through with the College, Rura. Shit on the novices forever. I got myself a transfer. Big wangle."

"So?"

"Don't you want to know where I've transferred?"

"You'll tell me, dear Kayt. You'll tell me."

"The Border Regiment!" Kayt was triumphant. "The Border Regiment. What about that, then?"

"Super," said Rura mechanically.

"All right, baby. Come to bed and be loved."

IX

KAYT AND Rura went up to Carlisle together. It was nearly five hundred kilometers from London—easily reached in half a day by gefcar. But there was no hurry. They had two full days before they had to report to the commandant of the Border Regiment. They traveled in a leisurely fashion, Kayt taking the wheel most of the time. If the weather was good—and it was—they planned sightseeing tours in the Peak District and the Lake District.

Once upon a time, long ago, a month ago, Rura had thought very little of pot, alcohol, tobacco—the social anodynes. She still did not care for pot or tobacco; but she had begun to lean heavily on alcohol. It was better than tranquillizers or sleeping tablets. It was more friendly. So she was content to let Kayt take the wheel and do most of the talking. Whiskey made her conversation seem interesting. Whiskey temporarily wiped out of Rura's memory the things she would always remember.

The fine summer weather continued. The whole of Anglia, it seemed, was bathed in sunshine; and it was pleasant to be idling across the country in a gefcar, without instructions to kill, without the need to do anything other than lean back and try to relax, try to forget.

They explored several ghost towns on the way. It was romantic to explore ghost towns, to listen for long-dead voices, to hear whisperings in the wind. Once the island of Britain had contained seventy million people, in the days before the Dark Ages. Now, the Republic of Anglia contained about three million women. There were, perhaps, thirty thousand pigs left scattered through the Highlands. But they were being exterminated at a phenomenal rate; and, as Curie Milford had suggested, in the foreseeable future, the last man would die.

Rura shuddered. There was such an air of finality about the concept. The last man would die. Men were animals, pigs. But should they be wiped out completely? Could not some be kept in zoos, reservations? Could they not be allowed their sows, their piglets? Could they not be allowed to breed in—of course—a limited fashion? It would be a service to womanhood. Future generations would be able to observe their life-cycle— as a dreadful warning.

"I don't think we should exterminate all men," pronounced Rura, after passing through the ghost town of Derby, while the alcohol was trickling through her veins like a thin stream of fire.

"Ovaries alive!" exploded Kayt. "That is what you have been training for. For two years you have been specializing in the art of killing men. And now you say: Let them live."

"I didn't say that."

"Baby, if anyone else but me heard it, that's what they'd think you said."

"Do we have to wipe them all out?"

"If we don't, they'll try to wipe us out."

"There aren't enough of them."

"There could be," said Kayt darkly. "There could be sooner than you think. They have nasty habits."

"We could settle them on reservations."

Kayt laughed. "'The only good Indian is a dead Indian.' Seriously, sweet. Don't start voicing these peculiar sentiments when we get to Carlisle. The Border Regiment is rather strong on tradition."

Rura drank more whiskey. "Why did Derby become a ghost town?" The ruined buildings had seemed very sad. Sad, too, to see trees and shrubs growing through the moss-covered concrete roads where once streams of antique traffic had made endless and monotonous music.

Kayt shrugged. "For the same reason that four-fifths of the towns are ghost towns. We haven't got enough women to fill them. And, dammit, we don't want enough women to fill them. Let's get it all back to Anglia's green and pleasant land, as some poetess once said. I used to have a passion for ancient history, Rura. Do you know there were once fifteen million ground cars on this island, spitting out carbon monoxide and lead compounds. Half the population had chest diseases. That's the work of men for you. . . . In twenty minutes we'll be in the heart of the Peak District. Let's have lunch on top of Mam Tor. On a clear day, you can see the Irish Sea."

"But why Derby," persisted Rura. "Why not Leicester?"

"How the hell should I know?" said Kayt irritably. "Maybe there is better drinking water in Leicester. Maybe they drove the pigs out sooner. Maybe the women were better organized. . . . I'll tell you something.

We've just passed through what used to be the industrial heart of England—Coventry, Birmingham, Nottingham, Derby. Four centuries ago, the men would draw their wages every Friday. Then they would go home and fuck their women on Friday night and go out and get drunk. Then they'd come back and fuck their women some more. On Saturday, the performance was repeated. On Sunday, the men rested in bed while the women did the work and looked after the children. Many of the women had four or five children. They were old at thirty, decrepit at forty, worn out at fifty. The men didn't care. They could always get other women."

Kayt had to stop the gefcar. Rura was sick.

X

CARLISLE CASTLE, the home of the Border Regiment, stood south of the River Eden. It had endured change, enlargement, attack, destruction, and modification for well over two thousand years. Once it had been a Roman cavalry fort, once it had been a Saxon stronghold. Then, in the eleventh century, William Rufus gave it the permanence of stone. It was a scarred veteran of the Border Wars. Mary, Queen of Scots came as its guest and stayed as its prisoner. At the beginning of the nineteenth century, three-quarters of it were pulled down. A hundred years later it was renovated as the headquarters of the old Border Regiment—the Regiment of Pigs—that had raised sixteen battalions in the First World War and shed its blood in France, Flanders, Macedonia, Gallipoli. But by the end of the twentieth century, the old Borderers were dead. And two centuries later, after the Dark Ages, the new Border Regiment was born—a regiment of women. Or, as they proudly called themselves, the Monstrous Regiment. An elite that was dedicated to the extermination of men.

Carlisle Castle had seen it all, and had endured. There were still stones that William Rufus had laid. But the foundation stone of the restored extension had been laid by Curie Milford.

Kayt and Rura arrived late in the afternoon. Late sunlight slanted down on the castle, giving the old part —now no more than a museum—a fairytale quality, bathing the new extension in a light that made concrete blocks look briefly like weathered stone. Kayt had been to Carlisle before and knew the layout and many of the officers. She took Rura to check in with the adjutant, Sharl Martell, an old friend.

"Kayt! Long time no drink. How are you?"

The two kissed and playfully punched each other's breast.

"Sharl! We'll catch up on the drinking tonight. I've brought you a good one. Rura Alexandra."

Sharl looked at Rura appraisingly. "Silver nipple, I see. You must be good."

"Lucky," said Rura. "Just lucky."

"So is the third company," said the adjutant. "They lost two last week. You will be more than welcome."

"How are things?" asked Kayt.

"Busy enough. The pigs are still trying to push south. I have a theory that their gestation is three months instead of the usual nine. I also think they grow up at a corresponding rate. The more of them you burn, the more they come up out of the heather."

"Relax," said Kayt, putting her hand round Rura's shoulder. "Rura and I are the U.S. Cavalry. I trained her myself. She can smell a pig at five hundred meters."

Sharl Martell looked at her thoughtfully. "Rura and you?"

"Yes, that's it. Rura and me. We have something going. She's a main course."

"I could be kind," said Sharl. "The third needs another officer. Interested?"

"Sharl, you're a peach."

"You may have to bribe me."

"I'll bribe you. . . . Yes, I know I'm not supposed to frat with my own company juniors. But rules were made to be flexible. We work well together, and that's a fact."

"Tell you what," said Sharl, "I'll be good to you both. And remember that entitles me to credit. The third needs an ensign, also. In view of the silver nipple, I can recommend that—"

"Sharl, you have unlimited credit." She slapped Rura's back. "Ensign Alexandra. You were born—or was it cloned?—bloody lucky. We'll dine in mess together, and we'll share the same patrols."

"For Goddess' sake, keep it cool in front of the old woman," said Sharl. "Colonel Claire thinks discipline is the eightfold path."

"She shall have discipline," said Kayt. "Enough to keep her happy. Also, she will be much improved when the third starts burning the highest number of pigs. Last time I was on active service I made the spotter record two years running."

Sharl smiled. "It is not forgotten. That's why you made the Border Regiment when there's a waiting list."

"Good. Show us where we sleep, and then we'll freshen up while the champagne gets cool."

"You'll freshen up; but there will be no boozing tonight, sweetie."

"Why not?"

"The third and the fifth stand to at dawn. It's all happening in the Grampians. Intelligence says that

MacDiarmid has reared his ugly snout once more. He is supposed to be raising a force."

Kayt snorted. "Dirks and crossbows! What the hell!"

"I forgot to tell you," said Sharl. "He did the second a serious injury three days ago. One chopper, five gef-cars, nine exterminators. It seems he and a few of his herd managed to get hold of some lasers. Now he has more weapons. The pig has become interesting. Also dangerous."

"Lasers or not," said Kayt, "he will be merely an instrument of promotion. Well, Rura, love, we'd better get to our quarters and take it easy. Both of us will need to be in good form on our first patrol. If we can blood ourselves with this MacDiarmid creature, it will not go unnoticed in London."

Rura felt faint. She knew she ought to say something —she had made little enough contribution to the conversation so far—but there did not seem anything to say.

"She looks very white," said the adjutant. "Are you all right, dear?"

Rura nodded, not trusting herself to speak.

"It's the excitement," said Kayt. "Graduation, silver nipple, and now ensign. It's all happening for her. She only needs a good night's rest."

Rura, tightly controlled, allowed herself to be shown to her room. When she was alone, she fell on the bed and began beating the pillow with her fist. She didn't know why she was doing it. She refused to know. Thought itself was repugnant.

XI

THE WEATHER had broken again; and it was a gray drizzly morning. *The hell with summer,* thought Rura sadly. *This was to be the great summer for me. Womanhood and graduation. Olane, Moryn and I would have applied to operate as a team. We had it all planned. We were going to be gay, take life easy for a while, make the routine runs into picnics, treat pig-hunting like a sport.*

And now the party that never was is over. Olane and Moryn are dead, and Diarmid MacDiarmid, whom I should have killed when I had the chance, has destroyed nine more exterminators. They will be on my conscience forever. It seems everyone is right and I am wrong—the pigs must be wiped. Especially Diarmid MacDiarmid. While he lives, I am unclean.

So here I am with total strangers on a foul morning, about to hunt down a man who should already be dead. What would they do if they knew that I could have killed him and didn't? They would kill me. It was their comrades who died a few days ago, their Olanes, their Moryns. . . .

It was not entirely true that Rura was with total strangers. Her crew members had been introduced to her the previous evening. Robin Deyn and Mirage Mathilde—seasoned exterminators. They had graduated a year ago.

Robin was pilot of the gefcar. Mirage sat in the back with Rura, filing a mark on the butt of her laser rifle. There were seven such marks, each one representing a kill.

The gefcar's rotascreen spun raindrops away as fast as they touched it; but visibility was poor, at times only fifty meters, and the gefcar dawdled along at about sixty-five k.p.h. Somewhere above, invisible, the spotter choppers fought their way impotently through mist and low cloud. Somewhere above, Kayt would be fuming at the rapidly receding possibility of coming to grips with the MacDiarmid raiders.

"Pity it's such a lousy day for your first mission," said Mirage. "Still, the weather can change an awful lot before we get to Fort William."

"If we ever get as far as Fort William," put in Robin. "Weather reports are lousy. My guess is we'll be ordered to abort before lunch."

"It will clear up," said Mirage. "I have a feeling."

"Baby," laughed Robin, "it's a fool of a feeling. You ought to listen to the language from the choppers."

Mirage checked position by the map. "Glasgow about twenty kilometers ahead. Shall we go round or through?"

"Hang on. I'll check with Command." Robin radioed the flag chopper. Rura could not hear what she said. She was not even interested.

"Flag says all sky-spotting is out. Cloud banks extend two hundred kilometers north. Use own initiative. The fifth are calling it a day. One of theirs has piled into a tree and another has had an argument with a hillside. Lousy piloting, if you ask me."

"Hooray!" said Mirage. "I was all for writing it off, really. But if the fifth have chickened, let's go see what we can find."

"Right." Robin listened to the radio once more. "Five of our company are turning back. Ground hazards, not acceptable, they say."

"Sows!" Mirage turned to Rura. "What do you think, baby? Should we or shouldn't we?"

"Let's go on," said Rura fatalistically. "You only die once."

"That's my baby! Hear that, Robin? The infant has more than enough."

"I hear," said Robin. "So now we can operate independently. I'll want some good navigation, Mirage, particularly when we get to the high ground. Meanwhile, what about Glasgow?"

"Through," said Mirage. "What else? There's always the chance of a pig hunting metal. Besides, I like dead cities. They are romantic."

Glasgow was indeed a dead city. As the gefcar ploughed cautiously through the suburbs on medium lift, Rura became even more depressed by the rows of ruined houses, shops, factories, halls. Once many thousands of people—women *and* men—had lived and worked and died here. But now groundsel, convolvulus, nettles, dandelions, and daisies were reclaiming the concrete jungle.

Way back in the days when men were still being

cleared from the cities, Glasgow had seen some of the bloodiest fighting in the Liberation War. Casualties were so high on both sides that, when the men had finally been defeated and driven out, there were not enough survivors to hold even the center of the city. Besides, it was too vulnerable, too near the Highlands. It was not worth the garrison needed to defend it. So the women who were left had been evacuated and re-settled south in more secure areas of the Republic of Anglia. Occasionally, when Intelligence reported signs of activity, the Border Regiment would turn out in strength, surround the ruined city and work inwards, burning out the scavengers. But the results rarely justified the effort. It was now more than two years since Glasgow was last cordoned. For the most part, it remained a no man's land and a no woman's land—unsafe for either pigs or exterminators to enter.

The rain seemed to be getting heavier. Rura and Mirage held their rifles at te ready. If any pigs were scavenging in this weather, they must be feeling pretty desolate.

None of the bridges over the River Clyde were still standing; but that was no impediment to a gefcar. Robin crossed the river near the remains of George V Bridge, went up past the wreckage of the old Central Station and turned left along the pockmarked track of Argyle Street towards the old University complex. For reasons no doubt psychological rather than practical, the University was a favorite haunt of pigs. But as the gefcar hissed past the blackened walls, there seemed to be no indication of recent activity whatsoever.

Rura felt glad. She was in no mood for burning pigs. She was in no mood for anything.

"We've lost radio contact," said Robin. "The static is frightening. I can't raise Command at all."

"Who cares about Command?" Mirage's spirits seemed to rise as Rura's fell. "We are better on our own. Let's make it one hell of a hunt and get the only kill of the day. Then everyone will hate us."

"The hell with Fort William," said Robin. "The weather is no good for such a long patrol. Let's take a look at the lochs. The pigs have a fondness for camping by the side of a loch. We can go up Lomond, across to Tay and then swing south to take us back by Edinburgh. That gives us three reasonable chances. It's a long enough trip for this kind of weather. What do you say, Rura?"

"Fine by me. I'm just the new girl."

"Well, then. It's along the Clyde and up Loch Lomond. Keep your eyes skinned for smoke. On a day like this, they won't be expecting us. They'll think they can put up tents and have fires and hot meals."

The sky became darker and darker but visibility improved as the mist lifted. It was more like November than August. The gefcar sped along the gray waters of the Clyde, then turned north to the broad expanse of Loch Lomond. Rura felt cold, but not physically so. It was the coldness of misery. She had no right to be patrolling with these two high-spirited Borderers. She was a charlatan. She was the exterminator who had let MacDiarmid live.

A wind had risen. The waters of Loch Lomond were turbulent. Robin put the gefcar on high lift. They ate a light lunch as they patrolled.

It was Mirage who spotted the fires—on the east side

of the loch, below mountains whose peaks were shrouded in mist.

"Tally ho!" shouted Mirage. "Pigs at three o'clock. Two fires, four tents, I think. Range two thousand meters plus."

"Since we're on the water," said Robin, "they have to be blind not to see us, even in this weather. Let's go in fast and burn the whole area before we touch down." She swung the gefcar at a sickening angle, giving all the acceleration she could get. It leaped across the water. Mirage and Rura wound down the windows and poked their rifles out. Rain stung their faces. Cold air made them catch their breath. The range shortened.

"One thousand meters!" sang Mirage. "No movement. They are blind, deaf and drunk. They are fornicating with their sows. This is going to be the classic extermination run. Five hundred meters. . . . Rura, baby, you're a good luck gift. Two hundred and fifty meters."

Rura was shaking. Sick and shaking. *Why didn't they make a run for it?* she thought. *They must have heard us. They must have seen us. Why don't they make a run for it?* She was cold, but her hands were slipping with sweat and the laser rifle felt as if it weighed a hundred kilos.

The fires and the tents were on low ground. Behind them, perhaps a hundred meters away, was the edge of a forest of pine trees; and beyond that the mountains rose, bleak and dark.

They must have heard us. They must have seen us, thought Rura. *Why don't they run for the trees? Some of them might make it.*

But it was already too late.

"Open fire," called Robin. "Maximum power. I'll circle,

then you can sweep from all angles. We'll roast them in their tents."

Mirage was enjoying it. Great brief gouts of flame shot up from two of the tents. The gefcar had reached the water's edge and was skimming above the slowly rising ground, circling the encampment at a distance of fifty meters.

"What's the matter, Alexandra? Why aren't you firing?"

"I don't know. I can't! I can't!" called Rura desperately. Her hands wouldn't obey her. She was sweating and shivering. The rain felt oddly as if the heavens were weeping.

"Shoot, damn you. This will go on your record sheet."

"Screw her," laughed Mirage. "Baby isn't needed. I've got it all sewn up."

All the tents were now aflame, the rain hissing and steaming as wood, skins and cloth ignited. No pigs ran out.

Robin circled the encampment. Mirage kept on firing and laughing. The place became a brief inferno. Rura wondered dully if women and children were being cooked. As an exterminator, she was finished. She knew it.

Robin grounded. "Alexandra," she said harshly, "there'll be a court martial. Now get the hell out and help us inspect the ashes."

Mirage was already on the wet and smoldering grass, her rifle ready, her face twisted into a wolfish grin, oblivious of the rain, oblivious of everything but the smoke and dying flames.

Rura stepped out of the gefcar, felt the soggy ground

beneath her feet, smelled the terrible smell of burning. It was a dismal day, sad and gray. There was nothing left to live for. She was a total failure.

"Kill me," she said simply. "Make it look as if the pigs did it."

"Too easy," snapped Robin. "The Borderers prefer to make an example of women like you. Now make yourself useful, bitch, and look for bodies."

Rura threw down her rifle. She listened to her own voice, quiet and controlled, with amazement. "Kill me. Or I'll come and get you, and wrap that damned rifle round your neck." She walked slowly towards Robin.

Mirage suddenly shouted: "Pigs!" She lifted her rifle and began to fire towards the pine forest. She continued firing even after her face was burned away, even as she fell.

There was a whistling sound. Robin grunted and looked stupidly at the arrow between her breasts. She swayed a little, her mouth working as if she wanted to say something. Another arrow hit her in the belly. She fell backwards, threshed about for a moment or two, then lay still.

Rura stood there frozen. She would welcome the arrow, welcome the big burn. At least, it was death with honor. Her back was to the pine forest.

She stood still, gazing out over the loch. Was it better to die on a dark, wet day, or to die in sunlight with the sky blue and with birds singing? She did not know. It did not matter. The end was all that mattered.

"Turn round, hellbitch," said a voice. A man's voice. "How would you like me to stick my penis between your legs?"

70

Rura turned round and looked at the pig. Bearded. They were all bearded. Unkempt. Wild animals. Destroyers. But those who destroy destroyers are themselves destroyers. Somewhere there had to be an end.

"I want to die," she said.

He laughed. "Do you, now? I want you to live—for the amusement, instruction and gratification of my comrades."

Several pigs had now come out of the pine forest. Some were armed with bows, some with crossbows, two with laser rifles. They stood around her in a semicircle. They all looked the same. Bearded, unkempt. Was it for such as these that she had refused to fire?

No! Perhaps, then, it was for a woman and a boy.

"Strip her," said someone. "Let her feel the wet grass under her buttocks."

"How long will she last?" said someone else. "I'm open to bets."

Rura looked at the rifle she had thrown down. *If I go for it now*, she thought, *they'll kill me. And that will be an end. Not a good end. Not a good time. Not a good place. But one cannot choose these things.*

She dived for the rifle. She never reached it. Somebody kicked her. Somebody tore off her clothes. And then, for a while, she saw faces above her. Different faces, but all the same. And sometimes the pain between her legs was terrible, and sometimes it was just strange, even bearable. She heard herself grunt and moan. She felt the rain on her face, and was grateful for it. She felt hands on her breasts, teeth in her neck. And, there again, sometimes the pain was terrible and sometimes it was not. She felt lips against hers, and fought them

71

away. For a time. Then there was no fight left. Only dumb acceptance.

Mercifully, the changing faces became lost in a fog. And then nothing mattered any more. And darkness was all.

XII

The nightmare of humiliation and degradation continued. In the darkness, Rura heard somebody calling, far, far away. No, not calling. Grunting, moaning—like an animal. She felt a stinging sensation and opened her eyes. Somebody was slapping her face. And she was doing the grunting and moaning. Like an animal. Rura Alexandra, silver nipple, ensign of the third company of the Border Regiment. Rura Alexandra was making strange, subhuman noises.

She felt the rain. The slapping had stopped. She felt the rain on her face—blessed rain. She felt the rain on her bared breasts, on her belly, on her legs. She felt cold, but it didn't matter. There was not enough rain. There never would be enough rain to wash away what had happened.

"Wake up, hellbitch," said a voice. "Tell us how much you liked it."

She tried to speak rationally and couldn't. There was a stickiness in her mouth, a strange taste. She coughed and swallowed, and coughed again. Blood. She must have bitten through her lips. Somebody had.

"Kill me," she managed to say. "Kill me."

There was laughter.

"Kill me," mimicked a voice dreadfully. "I have been ravished, violated, raped by wild Highland pigs, and I do not want to give birth to a litter. Kill me—because I liked it, and my eyes popped and my tongue stuck out. And I might just want it again."

More laughter.

Another voice. "Get up, hellbitch, or you'll get the replay. Put on your pretty little uniform, what's left of it. Can you pilot the gefcar?"

"Kill me. Please." She did not want to beg, but she was begging.

Somebody put a foot on her breast. There were studs in the sole of his shoe. The studs cut into her flesh. She looked up past the tattered trews, the heather-colored tunic, and saw a face. Grotesquely foreshortened. The face, lined, bearded, seemed to sit just on top of a massive pair of legs. It was the face of man, the destroyer, the ultimate pig.

The boot twisted. Rura groaned. She stared stupidly as thin rivulets of blood trickled down from her breasts to merge with the falling rain.

"Can you pilot the gefcar?"

"Yes," she managed to say. "Yes!"

The foot was removed. "Then you are bloody well going to, hellbitch. Now, pull yourself together and put on your clothes. Anyone would think you'd been having an orgy."

More laughter.

Slowly, painfully, Rura lifted herself up. No one helped her. There was something sticky running down her legs. She tried not to think about it. She got to her knees. Naked. She looked at the men, looking at her.

Odd. They could meet her gaze. But she could not

meet theirs. Never had nakedness seemed so terrible. Someone handed her her tunic. Torn down the front. But the damned silver nipple was still in place. She didn't put the tunic on. She wrapped it round her and tried to stand. She fell.

There were cheers.

She fell on her face, and somebody kicked her bottom, not too painfully.

"No more of that," said a voice. "We'll preserve what's left. We must preserve what's left for the judging."

She felt hands on her shoulders, and flinched. The hands were firm but gentle. They helped her to her feet. They helped her put on her wet clothes, wipe the mud from her face. She did not dare look at the face of the man who was helping her. She was afraid of what she might see.

"You're going to pilot the gefcar, hellbitch. You're going to take a journey. You're going to see the laird."

She was propelled towards the gefcar and thrust into the pilot's seat. Two men sat behind her. She felt the barrel of a laser rifle at her neck.

"Don't reach for the radio," said a voice. "We wouldn't like it. We wouldn't kill you, of course. Only half-roast you. It would be very unpleasant. You understand?"

She was shaking and shivering. Shaking with fear and shivering with cold.

"I'm in no shape to pilot this thing," she said desperately. "Can't you see? I can't even hold the damned stick."

"We wouldn't want you to crash, either," went on the voice. "We'd still scorch you, among other things. However, we are reasonable men, sometimes. Take a drink of this. Let it get into your blood. Then we'll lift off."

A small flask was handed to her. She didn't care what was in it. She just drank, gratefully. Whiskey. It burned and made her cough. She drank some more, swallowing it as if it were water. Presently, her limbs began to tingle; but the shaking and shivering stopped.

The one thing not to do, Rura told herself, *is to think. Thinking has destroyed me. Wherever I go, whatever I do, I carry with me now the anticipation of death. Therefore, do not think.*

"Well, Madam Exterminator, you have run out of time. Lift off and head up the loch. I'll navigate for you. But, if it's any help, I'll tell you where we are going. We are going to Tobermory on the island of Mull. It's an inhospitable place, is Mull. There's nothing on the island worth having, nothing to merit the attention of your Monstrous Bloody Regiment. Which is why the laird chose it. Mull is probably the end of the road for you, hellbitch. Try to get there without having your breasts burned off."

Obediently, Rura lifted the gefcar and swung out into Loch Lomond. The sky was darkening, the rain was heavier. The rotascreen whirled the raindrops away; but visibility was very poor, and the water was choppy.

I could cut the lift, and drown us all, thought Rura. *That would be an end to it. My body cleansed in the waters of the loch, and the bones of these two pigs to whiten by the side of mine.* She shuddered, but she did not cut the lift. Perhaps, unconsciously, she was seeking a more dreadful death, a more dreadful humiliation.

"Swing to port," said one of the pigs. "There's a valley that goes round Ben Lui and leads to the top of

Loch Awe and then the leaward end of Loch Etive. And after that, we can have a switchback ride up the Sound of Mull. Do you get seasick hellbitch?"

She didn't answer. She just followed the commands like a robot. Rura Alexandra, silver nipple, was submitting to the commands of a dirty pig. Every picture, as they say, tells a story.

Loch Lomond was behind. Mountains loomed, vague, mist-shrouded. Mountains and glens. Then there was more open water. The pigs seemed to know what they were doing, where they were going. Rura didn't care any more. There was nothing to care about. Finally, they came to the sea. Rura hardly noticed. The swell was heavy; and that is how she knew it was the sea. But it didn't matter. Nothing mattered any more.

The rain was very heavy indeed in the Sound of Mull, and the sky dark.

It looks like the end of the world, thought Rura. *Well, it is the end of the world for me. I am twenty years old and about to inherit an eternity of nothing. Perhaps there can be ghosts. I hope not. How would I ever explain to Moryn and the others?* She switched on the gefcar's single, penetrating headlight; but she was immediately ordered to cut it.

"I don't think you have choppers aloft, hellbitch. And I don't think they could spot anything if you had. But let's not tempt fate. The laird would not like it."

"I can't see," she said.

"Don't worry, screwmeat." There was laughter. "Don't worry about trifles. We are your eyes."

Rura could see nothing but rain and wind-whipped water. Yet the two pigs seemed to know exactly where they were. They guided her up the sound and made her

beach the gefcar by the ruins of the village of Tobermory. They made her cut engines and ground. Then
they used the headlight to signal.

Figures appeared out of the mist and the rain. Rura
was dragged out of the gefcar and flung on the stony
beach. A man came and looked down at her. She could
see his shoes, such worn and battered shoes. But she
dared not look up.

"Greetings, laird," said one of the pigs, "we bring
bounty. A gefcar, three-quarters fueled, laser rifles,
grenades, and a hellbitch."

"Greetings, Fergus Mackinnon. The day, though poor,
has gone well for you, I see. Did we suffer casualties?"

"No, laird. The hellbitches took the bait. There were
no casualties. But we killed two, and took this one.
There was no fight in her."

"No fight in her. Interesting. The Border Regiment is
not noted for pacifism."

Suddenly, Rura knew the voice. Perhaps she had
known it as soon as she heard it. Perhaps she had not
wanted to recognize it. She looked up at the face of
Diarmid MacDiarmid.

XIII

IN THE village of Tobermory on the island of Mull, there were a few houses still standing. They were houses that had endured for the best part of four hundred years. They were made of stone and roofed with slate. They were primitive dwellings, and had the primitive quality of survival.

Rura was taken to one of them. There was a fire on a hearth that belched as much smoke into the room as was drawn up the chimney. Diarmid MacDiarmid sat on a chair that looked oddly like a throne. Rura stood before him. Behind her stood various men and women dressed in skins and woollen cloth.

"The judging," said a voice. "Let us have the judging."

Diarmid MacDiarmid looked at her. Then he looked at the people behind her. "There will be a judging," he said. "But I must declare my interest. I know this woman. Therefore, I surrender the seat of judgement to whosoever would claim it."

"None but you, laird. None but you!"

"I ask again. Does anyone claim the judgement seat?" There was no answer.

"Well, then, let none dispute my judgement."

Someone prodded Rura in the back. "Kneel before the laird, hellbitch."

"I will not kneel," said Rura. Her voice was no more than a whisper. With an effort, she raised it. "I will not kneel. You can beat me down, but I will not kneel."

There was laughter. "Good show!" "This one still has fight in her." "Accept the invitation, laird!"

"Silence!" Diarmid's voice had a cutting edge. The laughter and the murmurings stopped. The laird turned to one of the men who had brought Rura. "Jethro, how came you by this hellbitch?"

"Laird, it was a poor, miserable day; but we set up the decoy camp by Loch Lomond as you commanded. None of us expected to see the Borderers. Their choppers could not spot, and the day was terrible dreary. We were thinking of abandoning the operation when this gefcar came churning up the waters of the loch. It was too good to be true. A single gefcar and no chopper. So, I'm telling you, we heaped dry wood on the fires, sprinkled a drop of oil to help with the burning, and ran for the trees. Those fool hellbitches thought they had hit the jackpot. They brought the gefcar in, circled the camp and burned it. Then they made the sixty-four-thousand Euro mistake. They grounded and got out. There seemed to be some sort of argument. This one," he glanced disparagingly at Rura, "threw down her rifle. Then, laird, we let them have it. There were only three hellbitches. The two with weapons, we took out. But this one, she was like a statue. She just didn't care. So we let her live. It was a dull day, and we felt entitled to some amusement."

"She amused you?"

"Yes, laird, that she did."

"They raped me," said Rura unemotionally. "Your valiant followers threw me on the grass, tore my clothes off and had their amusement. I was told what men were like, I was told that they were pigs. Now I know."

Diarmid MacDiarmid ignored her. "Jethro, at any time did she attempt to kill anyone?"

Jethro laughed. "The lassie was dazed, dazed beyond comprehension. Stoned for all I know. Laird, she did not attempt to kill. She said she wanted to die. And that was funny. For a fact, that was funny."

Rura looked at Diarmid MacDiarmid. "How is your shoulder? Has it healed?"

"It is healing. . . . But there are things which do not heal."

Rura said coldly, "I have my own dead to mourn. If I had destroyed you when I had the chance, there would have been less of them."

"The judgement, laird!" shouted someone. "Let us have the judgement."

"Let her make love to a dirk."

"Give her to the men!"

"Hell, no. Give her to the women." There were roars of laughter.

Diarmid was unperturbed. "Enough," he said quietly. "Would you have this educated female think she is among savages?"

More roars of laughter.

Diarmid looked at Rura once more. "Do you know what happens when your people take prisoners?"

"Exterminators rarely take prisoners. We are trained to destroy."

"Nevertheless, Madam Exterminator, prisoners are taken. The lucky ones only have to enjoy the attentions of your comrades for a while. Then they are castrated and killed. The unlucky ones go to the death camps. Our women—if they are pretty—are sent to your brothels. If they are less lucky, they are used as breeding machines. Our children are simply used for target practice."

"You lie!"

"I do many things. But I rarely lie. Unless I have to. Here I do not have to lie. Here I am the laird."

"Judge her. The bitch must die. It is only a question of how she dies."

"Or lives," said Diarmid. "The judgement is mine." He looked at the men and women standing behind Rura. "For reasons with which I will not quarrel, you, my friends and companions, have come to trust me. More, you have chosen me to lead you in our ceaseless war upon the perverted society of women. Therefore, listen to what I have to say. This creature, Rura Alexandra, Exterminator of the Border Regiment, is our prisoner. Yet none here has seen her kill. None has seen her attempt to kill. And I have seen her decline to kill. As you know, I have recently lost my wife and my son. This exterminator was present. She did not participate in their deaths. She could have killed me, but she did not. Therefore, it is my judgement that she lives. Further, since I am without a woman she shall be my woman. And since I am without a son she shall bear one, restoring that which was lost. This is my judgement and my will. Are there any present who would challenge this decision?"

For a moment or two, there was an electric silence. It was ended as a dirk flew through the air and penetrated the wood of the chair on which Diarmid Mac-

Diarmid was sitting. The dirk hit the back of the chair a few centimeters from Diarmid's head.

"Laird, I challenge." The man who had thrown the dirk stood forward. He was a heavy, muscular man, dressed almost entirely in skins.

"Ah, the Douglas," said Diarmid. "You have long sought the leadership, have you not?"

"Ay, laird. I think I'm a better man for the work at hand."

"And this is your opportunity."

"This is my opportunity."

Diarmid MacDiarmid stood. "My judgement is challenged. The issue will be decided by individual combat, here and now."

"Laird," said the Douglas, "let us be reasonable. Give death on the hellbitch and rest awhile. I cannot fight a man still recovering from wounds."

"The dirk was your messenger," said Diarmid. "I declared my interest. The hellbitch will be my woman. We will fight before this company, and the leadership will be settled."

"No!" said Rura. "Kill me now and save more blood from being spilled."

"Be quiet, woman," said Diarmid MacDiarmid. "You speak too much."

"Laird, I will not fight now," said the Douglas. "Victory would be a shame I could not endure."

"Do you withdraw your challenge?"

"No."

"I am sorry. Truly sorry. Then we must fight."

There were a few seconds of uproar. "Withdraw, Douglas!" "Kill the hellbitch." "She divides us!" "Give her the death she deserves, laird!"

"Silence!" Again Diarmid MacDiarmid's voice was not loud, but it was effective. "The leadership is challenged. I will not stand down. I will not reverse judgement. If I die, the hellbitch dies. That is enough. If the Douglas triumphs, I enjoin you to loyalty."

The burly man who had issued the challenge did not seem too happy with the way things were going.
"Keep the woman for now, and let us decide this matter later."

Diarmid shook his head. "Bad thinking. That is how factions develop. Factions breed disloyalty."

"There is no need to fight," said Rura. "I—" Someone slapped her face. It was a heavy slap. She saw stars, and the skin tingled as if it were on fire.

"Be silent, hellbitch," said Diarmid. "You have entered a man's world. You have much to learn."

"The weapon, laird?" The Douglas looked at Diarmid anxiously.

"The dirk, man. What else? I only need one good arm for the dirk."

"Defeat or death?"

"Death only. You forget about factions, Douglas. Dead men cannot plot. Now let us go outside so that one of us may feel the rain for the last time."

They trooped out of the house. The rain was still heavy, but the sky was lightening in the east. Rura was held by two women. Their clothes were wretched. They stank.

The men formed a circle on rough ground not twenty meters from the sea. Waves roared on the shingle, and the wind blew noisily. It was a poor day for living, or for dying.

Diarmid MacDiarmid and the Douglas entered the

circle, each armed with a dirk, each with a plaid wrapped over his free arm.

"I call all here to witness," said the Douglas, "that the time and place were not of my choosing."

"I call all here to witness that I declared my interest, and none complained. Yet my judgement is challenged, and I defend it."

"You are ready, laird?"

"Yes, Douglas, I am ready. And the rain feels good upon my face."

The two men circled warily. The Douglas tried one or two feints. Diarmid was nimble, and not to be shaken.

"There is still time, laird, to end this thing amicably."

"Man, we ran out of time when you threw the dirk. How does the rain feel, Douglas? Does it feel good?"

Suddenly Douglas lunged. The arm with the plaid on it took his stroke. When he pulled the dirk back, there was blood on it.

"A touch! A touch!" shouted the onlookers.

Rura wanted to be sick. She was wrong, and everyone else had been right. Men were truly destroyers. With no one else to destroy, they would kill each other. She forced herself to look at Diarmid MacDiarmid. His teeth were bared, his lips fixed in a terrible grin. He was an animal.

"A touch, indeed," said Diarmid. "First blood to Douglas. Last blood—who knows?" He did not attack. He waited.

The Douglas sensed a quick victory and lunged again. Diarmid stepped aside, but slowly. The dirk ripped his shirt.

Now the Douglas was confident. His opponent was too slow. The touch had unnerved him. Now was the time for a quick victory. He would lunge again, and the laird would parry or step aside. And then Douglas would whirl, and the dirk would be in the laird's heart.

He lunged, expecting the parry.

Diarmid MacDiarmid did not parry. He leaped high. The dirk found his leg. But as he came down, his body seemed to stretch, his arm seemed to lengthen; and his dirk was buried to the hilt in the neck of the Douglas.

The big man swayed crazily, and his arms fell by his side. The dirk dropped from his fingers. Blood oozed from his lips. "One more for MacDiarmid," he murmured. "The rain—" Then he fell.

Diarmid stood for a while, breathing heavily. Then he looked at Rura. "Hellbitch, now you are truly my woman. Tend to my wound."

XIV

EVEN IN its most prosperous days, in the latter part of the twentieth century, the tiny seaport of Tobermory had never had more than a thousand inhabitants. Their stone cottages had hugged the bleak land and huddled together as if seeking comfort from each other for the eternal ravages of wind and sea. Now, the temporary population of Tobermory consisted of only a few dozen men and women and children. They would not stay too long. They did not stay anywhere long; because if they did, the exterminators would find them. Then the air would be dark with choppers, and there would be gefcars racing up the Sound of Mull—gefcars filled with dedicated women in black, intent upon delivering death by burning.

Diarmid MacDiarmid, as befitted his position, occupied the best of the cottages. It was, at least, weatherproof. Miraculously, the glass remained in two of the windows. The other three were boarded up.

After his duel with the Douglas, Diarmid—bloodsmeared and terrible to look at—had again inquired if anyone disputed his judgment. He looked formidable with the wind whipping his hair and beard, with his ripped shirt and with the blood dripping from his injured arm. There was silence among the group of people who had witnessed the combat. Not one of them had thought that he could survive. Truly, the man was superhuman. Some might disapprove of him; nevertheless they were proud of him. They were proud that the laird was a man beyond ordinary endurance.

The Douglas was stripped of his clothes and weapons —both of which were precious—and Diarmid supervised the sharing-out. Then the naked body was thrown into the raging sea, to disappear rapidly in the swift ebb tide.

Satisfied that matters had been conducted fairly according to custom, Diarmid turned to Rura. "Take me home, hellbitch. It is but a few paces. I have whiskey and bandages, and I have need of both."

He put his arm around her shoulder and leaned heavily on her. Rura said nothing. She followed his directions and took him to his cottage. When the door was closed behind them, he uttered a great sigh and fell into a wooden chair.

"Get the whiskey first. There's a cupboard in the kitchen; and, praise be, it contains a half-liter flask, nearly full. Bring two glasses. If you have been raped as much as you claim, you could probably sink a glass or two yourself."

"You are injured," said Rura. "What is to prevent me from killing you?"

He laughed. "Very little. But for fuck's sake get the whiskey. You can kill me when I'm pissed."

Rura found the whiskey and the glasses. When she came back, Diarmid was shivering. "I'm cold. There's wood for the fire. Make it a big one. This is an occasion. I doubt that your comrades will come looking for smoke.

But if they do, what the hell? I'm tired."

Rura got the fire going while Diarmid poured drinks. He drank some whiskey, uttered a sigh of contentment, and poured more. "Was it bad, Rura Alexandra?"

"Was what bad?"

"The encounter on Loch Lomond."

"Bad enough. I would have preferred to die."

Again he laughed. "Death before hishonor. That's showbiz for you. Spare me the details. I do not wish to know how many men have had my woman before I have."

"I am not your woman!"

"Drink some whiskey, Rura Alexandra. You are my woman. This day, I fought and killed for you. We could not afford to lose the Douglas. But I fought and killed. You are my woman."

"I'll kill *you*!"

"Probably. But you are my woman. Drink."

She drank. The whiskey tasted terrible and felt wonderful.

"Life," said Diarmid, pouring more whiskey, "is full of surprises. You were present when my wife and son died. You remember?"

"I remember."

"I hated you then."

"I hate you now."

"We shall have to see about that." He groaned. "Damn this bloody arm. It has taken too much punishment recently." He tried to hold it out and couldn't. The blood dripped between his legs.

"Shall I clean it and bind it for you?"

"Not yet. Drink more whiskey, and decide whether you should kill me."

Obediently, Rura drank. She was glad of the whiskey and glad of the fire that was beginning to burn. She was still feeling dreadfully cold. "What do you usually do with women you take prisoner?" she asked unsteadily.

"Ah, well, that is a double question, you see. Usually, we divide them into two classes—women and exterminators."

"You don't consider exterminators to be women?"

"Demonstrably not. What woman in her right mind would dedicate herself to killing men?"

She sighed. "You avoid answering."

"I do not. We are short of women. We are always short of women. We raid for them. Often we can get rid of this homosexual nonsense they have been taught, pretty damn fast. Your society has brainwashed them into thinking that lesbian love is the greatest, but their bodies know different. And their bodies learn very quickly."

Rura shuddered. "That, too, is brainwashing."

Diarmid laughed. "Not brain. Breasts and vagina. Brain was quite a late appendage in evolutionary development. Impregnate a woman, Rura Alexandra, and she undergoes a remarkable change. Brain counts far less than belly. You exterminators can burn men. But you can't burn biology. Give me some more whiskey. You wouldn't want to kill me while I was still sober, would you?"

She refilled his glass and her own. "And what of exterminators?"

"Cheers! Exterminators. Well, they are not quite women, and they are not quite not women." He gave a bitter laugh. "We have become a crude people, Rura

Alexandra. We have seen too much death. Exterminators derive their strength from a philosophy of destruction. If we take them alive—which is not often—we generally grant them their death-wish, after the men have amused themselves."

Rura flung her glass down. "Pigs! Savages! Sadists!"

He smiled. "Men, also. . . . Tell me, did your late friend not enjoy killing my son? I am interested. Tell me."

"That was . . . it was different."

"So?" Again he laughed. "You have much to learn. I will teach you. I will teach you in the heather and in the bed. You will learn what it is like to be a woman. Who knows—you may even bear me a son."

"Pig! I will never lie willingly with you."

"Then you will lie unwillingly, or you will kill me." He took out his dirk and threw it at her feet. "You are trained, you have a weapon. I am injured, I have none. Now is your opportunity. While the whiskey makes fools of us both, now is your opportunity."

Rura looked at the dirk. She picked it up. There were still smears of blood on it. Blood of the Douglas.

"Give me another drink," he said tranquilly. "I am tired, but oblivion is always a hard thing to face."

She poured the drink and gave it to him. She did not let go of the dirk.

"Cheers, Rura Alexandra. I am but a filthy beast, and I have killed for you. Perhaps it was a mistake which you are about to rectify."

He put the glass down and gazed at her. In desperation, Rura lunged with the dirk. Almost negligently, he slapped her arm away. The dirk rattled to the floor. Rura fell against him in the chair.

"I love you," she said, not knowing what she was saying. "I love you." Her head lay on his chest. She felt immensely tired. She could smell sweat and blood and rain-drenched clothing.

He stroked her hair. "People," he said, "are the damndest thing. I think we need each other, you and I. It's the saddest joke in the world."

XV

THE EVENTS of the day had piled up on Rura, until she became too exhausted, too traumatized, for coherent thought. Somehow she managed to clean Diarmid's wound and bind it. He had had to tell her what to do; and she had obeyed his instructions mechanically, like an automaton. The wound was not bad. The dirk had ripped the flesh, but there did not seem to be any serious damage to the muscle. Diarmid made her sew the lips of the wound together with needle and thread while he drank what was left of the whiskey.

Night came, bringing heavier rain. The wind and the rain whipped the walls of the cottage; but the fire on the hearth burned brightly, and there was a plentiful supply of wood. In the kitchen, Rura found a bag of oats, some concentrated milk and some strips of venison. Diarmid showed her how to dilute the milk to the right stength, boil the oats and make a porridge that was just about edible. Then he showed her how to roast strips of venison by the fire.

She did not feel hungry, and she found the food unpalatable. But, somehow, she forced it down, sensing her body's need.

Diarmid watched her with amusement. "Hot food," he

said. "This is luxurious living. Wait till we have to survive in the heather for days at a time, and no fires for cooking. You'll be surprised at what you can eat."

"I think I am beyond surprise," she said dully. "I am a traitor, and quite probably mad. I should have used the dirk on you and then on myself."

Diarmid gnawed at his venison. He ate it greedily like a wolf. And yet there was an odd dignity to his movements.

"What good would that have done?"

"It would have solved two problems, our problems."

"Ay," he agreed, "it would have taken us out of all the trouble. But you could have done it that day on the hillside, and you didn't. The life force burns in you, Rura, as it burns in me. We are both children of darkness who want to see the sunrise."

"Will there ever be a sunrise?"

"Probably not."

"Then why go on fighting? Why keep up this hopeless cause?"

"Because I am a man. I am not to be declared obsolete by a bunch of flat-chested homosexuals who think a dildo is a substitute for natural living."

"I loved women," she said with some defiance. "I still love them. I love them because they are gentle and graceful. They have a sensitivity, a perception, that is alien to men."

"Even exterminators?"

"Even exterminators. I was an exterminator. I know them."

"No, lassie, you were not an exterminator. Trained to kill, yes, but with no appetite for it. Your real exter-

minator, your professional, enjoys killing. It does something for her juices. It gives her the big orgasm."

"You are revolting."

"Yes, Rura, I am revolting. I am also an authority on
exterminators. I have seen many in action. I could tell
you things that would make you retch."

"I won't believe your lies."

"No need to. You'll see the truth soon enough. . . .
You said you loved me, Rura. Now why the hell should
you love me?"

She was confused. "I don't know. Did I say it? I
didn't know that I said it."

"You deny it, then?"

"I—I—" She began to cry.

"That's the thing, lassie. Tears are marvelous for
getting it out of the system. Let it all come. I wish I
could cry now. I truly do."

"Why couldn't you let me die?"

"Well, now, Rura, that is a nasty question. Yes, that is
a very nasty question. I could have tossed you to the
pack, but I didn't." Diarmid passed a hand over his face.
Suddenly, he seemed very tired. "Maybe it was because
you held my son in your arms. Maybe it was because you
laid him very gently by his mother. Or maybe there was
a brightness about you. . . . It doesn't matter. It
doesn't matter at all. We need each other, it seems, and
that is enough. Come, spread some rugs by the fire and
let us lie together and try to be warm. I will not ravish
you, nor will you use a dirk on me. We will sleep and
try to forget the world that destroys us both. Is that a
fair bargain?"

"Yes, Diarmid, that is a fair bargain."

During the night, Diarmid groaned and shivered and felt the pain in his arm. Rura held him close, soothing him, trying to keep him warm. It was a long night. The rain stopped a little before daybreak. Then Diarmid sank into a tranquil sleep. When he awoke, he seemed refreshed. Rura still felt tired. A great fatigue of the spirit. . . .

XVI

THE MORNING was bright, the air crystal clear. The sun
shone from an evenly blue sky. It was as if yesterday
—the yesterday of storm and darkness, of disaster and
degradation—could never have happened.

Under patient instruction, Rura had cooked salt
bacon and potatoes for breakfast. The meal was washed
down with spring water. It was a good meal. It helped to
combat the fatigue.

Rura inspected Diarmid's wound. It looked all right.
She could not understand how she had had the courage
to sew the flesh together as if it were no more than a
piece of torn fabric.

But stiffness had set in. Stiffness and pain. Diarmid
winced as she gently bathed his arm.

"I hope no one else is going to emulate the Douglas.
I don't think I'm in any condition to leap about with a
dirk in my hand. Rura?"

"Yes, Diarmid?"

"You can't wear what's left of that bloody uniform
any more. It's neither practical nor politic."

"I know."

He took a deep breath and tried to sound casual. "I
have Flora's bundle with me—Ewan's, too, come to

that. You'll find Flora's bundle in the kitchen. She never had much. There was never much to have. But there might be something you could wear."

"That is what you want?" She felt numb. This man was callous. How could he humiliate her like this? How could he treat her like an instant, disposable female? Because he was a pig, that was how. A pig without feeling, without imagination.

He saw the look on her face. "No, lassie. It's not what I want. Nor, I suspect, is it what Flora would want. It's simply what is necessary."

"It may be necessary to you," she flared. "It's not necessary to me."

"You are my woman, now."

"So?"

"So my necessities are yours."

"That remains to be seen."

He stood up and hit her. A flat hand hit. Not a slap. The teeth rattled in her hand, her face became instantly on fire, and she went sprawling.

"Rura Alexandra, understand this. Flora was a great woman. She endured much. She did not complain. She carried her child across the length and breadth of Scotland through many an action. She learned how to strip the dead, how to destroy the enemy. She gave milk from her breast to a comrade who was dying of hunger. Finally, she gave her life for mine. Whan I ask you to wear her clothing, I do you much honor. Too much, perhaps. But Flora would have understood, even if you do not."

There were tears on his cheeks. Tears running from his eyes like rivulets, falling from the tip of his chin. Rura forgot her pain, her humiliation, and marveled at the tears. Pigs cannot weep.

"I'm sorry."

"Don't burden me with your sorrow, girl. I have my own. Look at the clothes. Put on something. The fit matters not. What matters only is that you shall be seen not as an exterminator but as a free woman."

"Are your women free, then?" She regretted the words as soon as she had said them. She did not regret the question, only the timing. One should not hit a man who weeps, even if he has struck first.

"They are free to be women. That is enough."

Rura picked herself up. "Last night you said you wished you could cry."

"It seems my wish has been granted. Take satisfaction from my weakness. Enjoy it fully. I doubt if you will see it again."

"I have never seen tears in the eyes of a man," said Rura.

"Then learn something from them, hellbitch. Learn something."

Rura went into the kitchen to open Flora MacDiarmid's bundle. It was such a sad little bundle. A shawl, two kilts, four tattered shirts, a pair of shoes that were falling apart, a metal comb, a mirror, a tiny bottle of perfume, a Celtic silver brooch, a square of silk, and a leather purse containing two neatly labeled locks of hair.

XVII

DIARMID HAD been listening to the radio, tuned to the Border Regiment's wavelength. He learned that Rura's gefcar was not the only one to be missing. Apart from known losses on the previous day's operation, one other gefcar had failed to return and had failed to signal its position. So a massive search was being mounted, a search that would extend throughout the entire range of the Grampian Mountains. The Border Regiment was on full alert; and all the lochs, valleys and glens would be covered. It was an opportunity that was too good to be missed. An opportunity to inflict further damage on the Monstrous Regiment.

Rura had put on a kilt and a torn shirt, the best of what she could find. She looked at herself in a cracked mirror and saw a wild Highland sow. What had happened to the neat exterminator? What had happened to the graduate with the silver nipple?

I am mad, she thought. *I have renounced civilization for barbarism. I have espoused a lost cause. Some day, not far from now, I shall die in the heather. My friends, my former comrades, will come with their certainty, their dedication, their laser rifles, and burn me from the face of the earth. And they will rejoice in my de-*

struction, in the death of a traitor. Why am I like this?
What is it that makes me betray my own kind, lie with
a pig, wear the uniform of slavery?

Diarmid stood in the doorway, watching her, reading
her thoughts.

"It is because you are discovering that you are a
woman," he said. "No more, no less. Women are not a
species, they are only part of a species. The war your
friends conduct is not against men, it is against nature."

Rura was amazed. "How did you know what I was
thinking?"

"The look in your eyes. The way you held yourself.
A woman would not have known, but I knew. There is
a fine tuning between men and women, Rura. There can
never be the same kind of tuning between women
and women."

"What do you know of women—real women? You
have only ever known—" She stopped.

"Wild Highland sows?" He gave a grim laugh. "They,
too, have breasts and soft flesh and rounded limbs. They
are thin because they are often hungry, they age quickly
because there is much to age them. But they are women,
real women. Sometimes, they are lucky enough to experience something of love. They bear children, perhaps
find a brief fulfillment, then they die. I have seen
them living, loving, bearing, dying. I know about
women. . . . The clothes sit well on you—better than
the black fabric of death."

"I—" Rura faltered. "I think she hates me. I—I could
feel it when I put on her clothes."

He shook his head. "All that is left of Flora is inside
me. That Flora does not hate you—only the world that
made you. All you have to remember is an anguished

woman with a dirk. But I have more, much more. . . . Lassie, this will not do. This kind of talk is for when the nights are long and the rain beats down and there is a fire to ease us into slumber. But now the morning is bright, the Border Regiment drives north, and there is much to be done."

"What do you mean?"

"I have been listening to your radio. Yours was not the only gefcar to be missing. Perhaps my people took out the other one, perhaps not. Anyway, the Borderers are coming north, and we must do our best to welcome them. We have your gefcar, and we have something better than crossbows. We are going to try to make your people understand that it can be expensive to venture into the Highlands."

"You'll need a pilot. Do you have a good pilot?"

"Yes, Rura, we do. We have you."

She gazed at him incredulously. "You expect me to pilot the gefcar so that you can destroy more of my comrades?"

"Exactly that."

"I won't do it."

"You are my woman. I fought for you. You love me. You will do it."

"I will not do it."

Diarmid sighed. "So the Douglas died for nothing. Let us understand each other, Rura. I fought and killed for you. You must adjust to our primitive psychology. You are my woman. I am the laird of a clan. If you will not do this thing, I will not kill you. I will give you to the clan. What they will do to you is something I do not care to think about greatly, though I have seen it before. You will say they are animals, and so they are.

So are we all. Animals have a right to survive, if they can. You are a link—quite a strong one at the moment —in their chain of survival. So you will pilot the gefcar, or you will soon be wishing that the Douglas had won and that you had been granted an easy death."

"Do you feel nothing for me?" she cried. "Doesn't it matter to you what happens to me?"

"It matters," he said. "It matters a great deal. But my duty is to serve my people, to look after their interests, as well as I can. There are no rules of war. Chivalry belongs to an age when the human race was not in jeopardy."

"Did I say I loved you?" she screamed. "It's a lie. It's a bloody lie. I lied to myself. There is no one to love, nothing to live for."

Diarmid gave a bitter laugh. "We live to endure pain, or we live to avoid it. In your case, you are now living to avoid it. You will pilot the gefcar."

"Soon," said Rura quietly, "I will kill you and then I will kill myself."

"Very likely. It was a thought that occurred to me the moment I saw you on Mull. It will be of little consequence. Meanwhile, you will take some of us back to Loch Lomond, and we shall try for a repeat performance."

XVIII

YESTERDAY LOCH LOMOND had been dark, hostile, turbulent. Today it was a lake of great beauty, calm blue waters under a calm blue sky, islands that looked as if they had been painted into the scene by a nineteenth century Romantic, mountains clothed in the rich, subtle hues of summer.

Yesterday Loch Lomond had witnessed death and savagery, the degradation of the human spirit. Would it witness the same again today? Would it always be like this until the last man was dead?

Rura was tired, desperately tired. Not just a fatigue of the body, but a fatigue that permeated her entire being. She had no willpower left, no resistance, no anything. It was as if she were an automaton. As if Diarmid —no, not just Diarmid, but all that had happened since Extermination Day—had swamped her, taken control of her, turned her into a creature without conviction, without purpose, without independence.

She had brought the gefcar back to that burned-out camp of death. She had brought the gefcar with Diarmid and two of his ablest men, armed with laser weapons and grenades. She wanted to be sick. It was all going to happen again. She knew it was going to happen. The meeting of hate with hate; the dreadful, senseless burning.

The burnt grass and the ashes of the tents remained undisturbed. Mirage and Robin lay as they had fallen. Mirage on her face, her head half-burned away; Robin on her back, an arrow between her breasts, another arrow in her stomach, and flies crawling over her sightless eyes. It was obscene. Must death always be obscene? Perhaps always if it was death by violence, death by hate.

Rura got out of the gefcar, made the mistake of going close to her companions of yesterday, and was violently sick.

Forgive me, she pleaded silently, as she retched, as her body convulsed, as the tears fell from her face and mingled with the vomit. *Forgive me, Mirage, Robin, as I forgive you. We all became caught in the dreadful machine of destruction. We do not make war upon men, nor they on us. We all make war upon ourselves. That is what we are driving ourselves to—racial suicide. So much for our fine ideals. It is a lovely day, though you do not know it. It is a lovely day, and you lie horribly dead, and there is more death to come. Forgive me. I shall join you. If not today, then some day soon. But the sun will continue to shine, the birds will still sing, and perhaps in the end the earth will be clean once more. Forgive me. We are all guilty, though our guilts are different.*

Steam rose in the sunlight from the vomit. There was not even any dignity in suffering.

Diarmid ignored her. He was busy briefing his companions. The gefcar was to be left visible by the camp. Rura was to be a decoy, a tethered goat. They stripped the body of Mirage—such a pale, slender body. Then they drew the tunic over Rura's head. Diarmid guided her arms into the sleeves. She submitted, limp as a doll, her eyes seeing nothing, her face expressionless. They tied her hands and hobbled her legs. She sat on the grass near the gefcar.

Diarmid came to sit by her. "I trust you," he said, "but they don't. I need their confidence."

"For this," said Rura, not looking at him, "I will hate you for ever." The taste of vomit was still in her mouth, a sour, bitter taste.

Diarmid sighed. "Love and hate. Each begets its own kind of violence, its own kind of misery. . . . Do you want a drink of water?"

She did, but she said, "I want nothing. Is it not enough to degrade me? Why must you make me play the traitor yet again?"

"You are no longer an exterminator, Rura. Therefore you cannot betray them."

"A fine piece of logic! It will help me to sleep well."

"Pray for miracles," said Diarmid. "Or what is left of mankind will sleep well, soon enough. Do you know what I want most of all? I want such a simple thing. I want a world where men and women can look freely and happily at each other, where they can enrich each other, where each can give to the other something beautiful. I am mad."

"Yes, you are mad. . . . I would like a drink of water."

He got up, went to the gefcar and brought her an old glass bottle—old because the glass was scratched, made frostily opaque, as if its surface had been sand-blasted. She drank from it greedily. The water was warm, but it tasted sweet. Wonderfully sweet.

"This bottle," said Diarmid, "is something of a talisman. I found it one day, years ago, on the seashore. I was thinking of killing myself. I was thinking of wading into the sea and swimming west, until I could swim no more. Then I saw the bottle, brought in by the tide. It had a stopper, a piece of cork. The bottle bobbed about, to and fro, until finally it was beached—almost at my feet. There was something inside it. I took the cork out, and I poked into it with a thin piece of wood. This is what I found." He took a folded piece of paper out of his pocket and gave it to her. "Read it."

The paper was old and stiff and stained. Rura held it in her tied hands. It felt as if it might crumble at her touch; but she managed to unfold it.

"To you," she read, "stranger and friend I shall never know, I bequeath one worthless thought from one worthless mind. We came from the dark, and into the dark we must all go. While there is light, love someone, believe in someone, try to achieve something. Men and women are transient creatures, but mankind abides. The flower, the fruit and the seed are one. Cherish the flower, ripen the fruit, and spread the seed. Stranger, I have nothing more to say—except that you are my sister, my brother, my friend."

Diarmid took the paper, folded it very carefully and put it away. "No signature," he said. "Who was he—or she? What had happened? It does not matter. Today, with luck, Rura, we shall destroy some of our sisters. I shall be glad to weaken the enemy, sad to kill people. It does not matter. All that matters is that mankind should abide."

One of Diarmid's men was sitting in the gefcar. The

hatch was open, and Rura could hear an odd, high-pitched voice.

"What is he doing?"

Diarmid gave her a wintry smile. "Fergus is a great female impersonator. He is transmitting a distress call. I do not think we shall have long to wait."

XIX

THEY CAME up the loch at high speed—two burnished, metallic beetles, racing to their destruction. There was a chopper with them. The chopper circled lazily at an altitude of perhaps five hundred meters.

Diarmid crouched in the gefcar. The two other men had blackened themselves and lay sprawled in the ashes of the camp, reasonably camouflaged as dead pigs. But they were pigs capable of an instantaneous and devastating resurrection with laser rifles and grenades.

There was no breeze; and already the air smelled of impending death. Rura had only seconds in which to do something. But what was there to do? Her hands were tied, her legs were hobbled, she had no weapon, Diarmid was between her and the radio. There was only one thing to do. Run to the water's edge, gesticulate, try to warn the gefcars away. Diarmid needed the element of surprise. If he or his men killed her, the gefcars or the chopper would see it. If they did not kill her, there was a chance.

But if she managed to warn the gefcars, that would probably be the end of Diarmid MacDiarmid. Please goddess, it would also be the end of Rura Alexandra.

Life was worth nothing when the only possibilities were kill, be killed, or betray.

Rura began to run. Stupidly she forgot about the short rope around her ankles. She fell down. Somehow, she picked herself up and began to shuffle to the edge of the loch in the tiny, grotesque steps the rope allowed. She waved her bound hands, hoping the gefcars would interpret the gesture correctly, hoping they would see that she was tied so that she could hardly move.

Any moment mow, she thought, *my head will be burned off. Any moment now there will be everlasting peace.* But perhaps Diarmid had planned it this way. Perhaps he wanted her to do something like this. Perhaps he thought it would distract attention from the trap. She couldn't think any more. She couldn't think. She fell down once more, picked herself up, waved, tried to run, fell down again.

She lay on the ground, winded, watching the gefcars execute a stylish turn, skim in from the loch and up towards the burned-out camp. Time seemed to slow down, almost to freezing. The chopper hung in the sky like a giant bird of prey. The gefcars touched down, a few meters away from her, spewing out the black figures of Border exterminators.

"Go back!" screamed Rura. "Get out! Get the hell out!"

The noise of the chopper and the dying gefcar engines swallowed her voice.

And then it was all transformed into stills, a series of photographs, each picture taken, developed, destroyed, second by second.

There was a girl with lovely blonde hair. First out of the first gefcar. An eager girl, swinging her laser rifle, surveying the camp, registering everything. Snap one. Then the others tumbled out after her. Snap two. Then they came out of the second gefcar. Snap three.

"Go back! Go back!"

It was too late.

The blonde hair flamed, the face blackened and steamed. A cry of anguish was burned out of an already dead throat. Borderers fell, cut, burned, contorting. The nightmare of destruction unfolded. One gefcar exploded. The chopper registered all, zoomed high, hovered, waiting, watching.

The air was choked with the smell of burnt flesh. Rura wanted to be sick again, but this was no time for luxuries. She got to her feet and tried to signal to the chopper.

She was rewarded with laser fire. The earth close by her became luminous, shooting gouts of flame and smoke up into the clear sky. She fell, coughing, retching.

One of Diarmid's men stood up and tried to blast the chopper. He was instantly beamed to oblivion. The other one was luckier. He managed to fire first, before he, too, was beamed. There was a different sound from the chopper's motor. Before, it had droned. Now it throbbed. The chopper gained height briefly, tried to pull away. Diarmid came out of the gefcar with his rifle. Coolly, he sighted the chopper. It exploded and fell like a stone into the loch. The last snapshot was a great splash. Globules of water in sunlight. Rura fainted.

She felt coolness on her face. Wetness. Water. The water of life. She wanted to be disappointed to find herself still alive. But she was glad. Glad and ashamed. She opened her eyes.

Diarmid had carried her to the water's edge and was

bathing her forehead. She sat up too suddenly. The world began to spin. She fell back and lay staring up at a dark cloud. No, it wasn't a dark cloud. It was Diarmid's face against the sky.

She saw the snapshots again. Blonde hair on fire. Bodies falling, burning.

"Murderer! Bloody murderer!"

"It's as good a word as any," he said softly. "To kill is to murder, to destroy the unique miracle of a living person. I only murder those who are trying to murder a species. Which, then, is the greater crime?"

Rura found that her hands and legs were free. Diarmid's rifle lay near—near enough to snatch, perhaps.

He read her thoughts. "You will have many opportunities to kill me. You are my woman. I cannot watch you always. I cannot be always awake when you are awake. Do you know what I am going to do now? I am going to bathe in the loch. A stupid thing to do, because the chopper had time to radio before I took it out. A stupid thing to do, because you are here and this place is littered with weapons. Rura Alexandra, you have wavered and wavered and wavered. You destroy yourself by indecision. Make up your mind, child. But let me have my swim first. The rain felt good when I had to kill the Douglas. The waters of Loch Lomond will feel good whether I live or die."

He began to undress. She watched him. While he was taking off his trews, she grabbed the rifle.

Rura got to her feet. "Murderer!"

"Just so. I am a murderer. Is a murderer permitted to swim before he is executed?"

He stood naked in the sunlight, facing her. She looked at the shape of his body, at the strength in those brown shoulders, at the scars that were not yet healed, at the gash in his leg, at the stitches in his arm—stitches that she had made. And at the strange male thing that hung between his legs.

"Murderer!"

"Well, then, Rura. Will you be a murderer also? It will not be too long before the Borderers come. My body will be a certificate of loyalty. But let me swim first."

He turned and walked into the water.

She tried to make her finger press the trigger. It would not. She cursed and wept. Then she flung the rifle down and began to tear off her own clothes. She refused to think any more. The time for thinking had passed.

Naked, she followed Diarmid into Loch Lomond. The water took her breath away. It was so cold. Colder than she had imagined. She rejoiced in the coldness, striking out into deep water, following Diarmid.

"I love you," she said. The water made her gasp and cough. "I love you, and I do not want to think any more. Diarmid, help me. Stop my brain from thinking. Stop it somehow."

He swam towards her, touched her, held her. "I can't stop you from thinking, but I can open the door to feeling."

He kissed her, and they both sank below the surface. Then they were coughing and spluttering and driving upwards once more.

"Let's go back," he gasped. "Let's go back. Now I know you are truly my woman, and we must both live. Let us get away from here before the women from hell come to claim us."

They swam to the shore, and lay there for a few minutes, letting the sun and the air dry them.

"Love me," said Rura. "I want to open myself for a man. Love me, please. This placed is filled so much with death. Let us leave it a few memories of life."

Diarmid lay upon her, caressed her, loved her.

It was not like the rape of the previous day. It was not like lying with women. It was not like anything she had ever known.

It was warm, it was disturbing, it was exciting, it was humiliating, it was proud.

She began to cry. "Isn't it strange?" she sobbed. "I don't feel afraid any more. The loneliness has gone, and I don't feel afraid."

XX

AFTERWARDS THEY had scudded away, up the narrowing waters of the loch, at high speed. Away from the place of death and destruction and love.

One of the Borderer's gefcars was damaged, but the other was untouched and still almost fully fueled. Diarmid chose it in preference to Rura's gefcar, which had now used up more than half its fuel supply.

While Rura had dressed once more in the faded clothes of Flora MacDiarmid and had done her best to dry her hair, Diarmid went on a grim tour of the corpses, collecting undamaged weapons and piling them in the back of the gefcar. Finally, he had destroyed Rura's vehicle and the damaged one with grenades. There would be little left when the next exterminator patrol arrived. Perhaps they would be willing to buy the idea of mutual annihilation. Perhaps not. It depended on what information the chopper was able to send before it was blown out of the sky. Anyway, it was worth a gamble. Diarmid burned two or three of the corpses to make them unidentifiable. Fortunately, a faint breeze took the dreadful smell of burning flesh away from Rura, lifted it above the trees, dissipated it among the hills.

Diarmid had called her when he was ready, and she

had walked to the gefcar, trying not to look at anything. She did not want to endure the agony of knowledge. She was committed now to the survival of man. Or was it just a man? She didn't want to know. She really did not want to know.

As the kilometers fled by, Diarmid relaxed. He had expected a rapid investigation. It had not happened. Maybe the chopper didn't have time to give an accurate reference. Maybe the nearest patrol was too far away. It didn't matter. What mattered was that he and Rura were heading north at maximum speed; and every minute that passed without a chopper in the sky or a gefcar on the loch increased their chances of survival.

What mattered to Rura, now—not thinking about tragedy or treachery or death—was the miracle that had happened inside her. It was like coming out of a dark tunnel into sunlight. It was like snow disappearing in a sudden thaw. It was like seeing the sea for the first time.

One part of her piloted the gefcar, efficiently, mechanically. The other part of her glowed. A man—this man by her side—had washed away twenty years of conditioning. He had loved her; and while semen had pulsed excruciatingly, wonderfully, through her vagina, she had seen the look in his eyes and had known the dissolution of Rura Alexandra and Diarmid MacDiarmid. There had been left only man and woman. Not man the rapist and woman the sex object. Just man and woman. Nature, throbbing with joy. Nature, goddess of seasons and harvests. Nature, mistress of life and death and birth.

Rura no longer believed in the supremacy of women. Nor did she believe in the supremacy of man. She believed only in the inevitability of life. The natural fulfillment of living things.

"Diarmid, where are we going? Do you want me to turn west for Mull?"

He shook his head. "We have paid a price, Rura. We have bought the rest of the day for ourselves alone. Turn northeast. We will go up Loch Tay and lose ourselves in the mountains. We will picnic and sun ourselves and pretend the world is young. Would you like that?"

She laughed. How as it possible to laugh after so much tragedy? She did not know, but she laughed. Perhaps it was just life rejoicing in life. "It will be a time to remember," she said. And suddenly, she was sad. "It will be a time to remember when there is no sunlight, and when all the horizons in the world are dark."

"Stop that, little one. Darkness there will be, soon enough. But before us there are the bright hours."

Loch Lomond was now behind, and the gefcar was riding over crystal streams through glens where the austere roll of the Highlands was exchanged for the richness of bracken, fern, rushes, wild flowers and grass that was luminously green. Ahead Loch Tay opened out, a kilometer wide, twenty-five kilometers long. Fish leaped in the sunlight. Salmon and trout. And the great stretch of water seemed to reach to the world's end. And the mountains on either side seemed like great breasts, heaving to the sky.

There was an island in the loch; and on it there were stone ruins, magnificent, beautiful, overgrown with creepers, eroded by time. The ruins of a priory, so Diarmid said, founded in the twelfth century.

Rura grounded the gefcar on the island. As the engine died, she sat still, listening to the silence. There was nothing but wind and sunshine and solitude. In a moment of clarity, she knew that she had arrived at the most beautiful place and the most beautiful time she would ever know on earth.

She got out of the gefcar and stood there, not weeping, but with tears streaming down her face. Diarmid put an arm around her shoulders.

"Each of us should have something beautiful to remember," he said. "Not many make it. We are among the lucky ones."

Suddenly she was jealous. "You brought Flora here?"

"There are many lochs in Scotland. There are many beautiful islands."

"You brought Flora here?"

"Yes, I brought Flora here."

"I'm wearing her clothes. Am I only a substitute? Are you trying to bring back the dead?"

His arm tightened. "I brought Flora here, and Ewan. You are wearing her clothes, it is true. But I am not trying to bring back the dead. The dead are gone for ever. . . . Let us go somewhere else. I do not want you troubled by imagined ghosts."

"No. We will stay. How did you love her?"

"Must we talk about Flora?" He sounded exasperated.

"Yes. How did you love her?"

"As a man loves a woman, that's all." His voice was hard. "I loved her tenderly. I loved her with desire. I loved her with sorrow. I saw her give birth and there was joy. I saw her die, and there was an emptiness. . . . Let us go now. The day turns sour."

"No," said Rura, tears still on her cheeks. "The day is not sour. I needed to understand, that is all. I, too, love Flora, because she loved you."

He went to the water's edge. "Ewan used to skim

stones. Sometimes, he could make the stone bounce five times."

"I can be like Flora," she said. "But I can never be like Ewan."

He held her against him tightly, so that she could hardly breathe.

"One day," he said with great intensity, "one day, you may give me a son. Not just a substitute for Ewan, as you are not just a substitute for Flora. But one day, perhaps, a son. Is it too much to ask?"

"I might give you a daughter. Would that matter?"

"I accept with love what is given with love. That is all there is to it."

"Then," said Rura, "accept *me*."

XXI

LOOKING BACK on those few hours—the bright hours—spent on the island in Loch Tay, Rura knew truly that they were the most wonderful hours of her life. Better than anything she could have imagined, far better than anything she had ever expected. She had found and enjoyed and savored the golden afternoon of her life. She was lucky, painfully lucky. So many lived and died without knowing the aureole of fulfilment, the afterglow of ecstasy.

It was a still afternoon—still and sultry, with a mood of impending storm. The storm would surely come. But meanwhile, the world was entirely beautiful. Such beauty was not to be wasted.

Diarmid caught trout in the shallows round the island. He stood in the water, his hands hanging loosely, until the unsuspecting fish came near enough for a strike. Then with one deft, practiced movement, he scooped the fish out onto dry land. Four trout danced a silvery saraband of death, then Diarmid came ashore and kindled a small fire.

The hell with choppers and gefcars. Somehow, Diarmid and Rura both knew that this was not a time for the angels of destruction. It was only a time for magic, for the short hours that are all that lovers can ever hope for.

The trout were cooked on forked sticks held patiently over the fire. Knives and forks and plates would have been incongruous. The fish were laid on leaves and delicately dissected by fingers. They tasted as fish had never tasted before. They tasted of stolen time.

Afterwards, Rura and Diarmid swam in the loch. Afterwards, they made love. It was an affirmation. And then they lay together, exhausted, staring at the sky, staring at the mountains, discovering the tracery of moss and lichens on the stones of the ruined priory, listening to the tangled sounds of flies and bees and heartbeats, knowing that each moment would be locked in the amber of eternity.

The sun began to sink over the hills. Diarmid sighed and sat up. "Rura Alexandra, I have accepted you. Do you truly accept me?"

"You must know the answer."

"I think I know the answer. But tomorrow, or the day after, I may have to kill again. I may have to kill those who were once your sisters, even your lovers. Can you accept that? There will be no end to it until men enjoy the rights of men once more, or until the last of us is burned out of history."

Rura was silent for a while. Then she said, "I have betrayed my friends. I cannot betray my race. Is that an answer?"

He kissed her. "It is a good answer. I doubt that you and I will die of old age, Rura. So let us remember and treasure what has passed between us. . . . Also, it is time that we returned to Mull. I recollect my duties."

Rura forced back the tears. "I am still discovering mine."

When they got into the gefcar, the magic of the afternoon was cut off as by a knife. The gefcar contained an assortment of weapons. It also contained an assortment of memories, bitter, terrifying. And somehow, despite airconditioning, it managed to retain the faint stench of burning. In her mind's eye, Rura could no longer see moss and ancient stones and silvery trout. She could only see human bodies, men and women, burned by hatred, obscene in death.

Diarmid sensed her mood and spoke only when necessary. The motors of the gefcar hummed into life. White-faced, and with automatic skill, Rura handled the controls. The machine lifted smoothly, swung away from the enchanted island and cut a long curve of turbulence across the smooth waters of the loch.

Diarmid acted as navigator. He did not need a map. He knew the hills and glens of Scotland as a man instinctively knows the lie of the country where he was born and has lived. He guided Rura across to Glen Lyon, over Rammoch Moor—desolate even in summer—and along the ancient road through Glen Coe, now almost entirely obliterated by grasses, bracken and small wild flowers, towards the sea.

It was in Glen Coe that Rura broke her depressed silence. "I remember the name," she said. "Something dreadful in Scottish history. Do you know what it was?"

Diarmid gave a faint smile. "The Glen of Weeping. Long ago, they used to call it the Glen of Weeping. It was the home of the Macdonald sept. Glen Lyon, which we came through, was, I think, the home of the Campbells. Six centuries ago, I think, it happened. The Campbells came to Glen Coe as friends, but backed by English guns. They asked for, and accepted, Highland hospitality.

Then, after two weeks, early on a winter's morning, they began to butcher the Macdonalds. Some of the Macdonalds fled to the mountains. But there was a blizzard, and most of them perished."

Rura shuddered. "The Glen of Weeping. It is a good name for such a bleak valley. Is there a happy end to the story?"

Diarmid touched her breast lightly, kissed her. "Rura, my love, happy endings are for children. No, there is no happy ending—just as there can be no happy ending to our story."

She looked at him, trying not to think of the laser rifles that lay behind them. "At least we have some happiness to remember."

"Yes, we are lucky. There are a few hours of which we can say: then we were truly happy."

The green-paved road through Glen Coe led down to Loch Linnhe and the sea. Waves broke on the stony beaches, golden in the western sunlight.

The Sound of Mull was little more than thirty kilometers away. Rura touched down almost by the sea's edge. "I want to breathe," she said. "I want to taste salt in the sea wind. Do you mind?"

"It is my pleasure also to taste salt in the sea wind."

They stood for a while on the beach, gazing to the west, inhaling deeply, watching the sun transform itself into a red ball, ready to drop over the edge of the world.

Rura shivered. "Soon the stars will be out. I love to look at the stars, but they make me afraid. They make me feel so small."

Diarmid laughed and put his arm round her. "What a strange pair we are. The stars give me comfort because they make me feel small. Come, we must return to Tobermory. My people have already stayed there too long, and tomorrow we must move. I am a bad general. I forget my duties. I forget that safety lies in mobility."

"Will it always be like this? Moving from place to place, never having time to make a home?"

"It will be like this in our lifetimes, Rura. We are the displaced people. We are the greatest lost cause the world has ever known. Your people—I am sorry, they are no longer your people—the masterful women, will not settle for anything less than extermination. We will not settle for anything less than parity for men. A lost cause, indeed."

"I am cold," said Rura. "Let us get back to Tobermory. At least we can hold each other there in front of a wood fire. How is your arm?"

"You have seen it. The muscles still work. It has held you."

"I was a fool. I should have let you rest."

"We are both fools, and we shall both rest soon enough. I am glad my arm still hurts. It reminds me that I am alive. To Tobermory, then. And tomorrow, we move."

They returned to the gefcar. Rura took it at cruising speed down the seaward reach of Loch Linnhe, past Lismore Island, and turned northwest into the Sound of Mull.

They knew something was wrong before they beached at Tobermory. Smoke rose from the island in straggling plumes. There were two wrecked gefcars in the village. There were two wrecked gefcars, and the silence of the dead. And the stench of burning.

Sea birds flapped and fluttered among the corpses. The Borderers had come and gone, though some had stayed.

The Borderers had come and gone, and there was nothing living left in Tobermory.

Diarmid's people had died with weapons in their hands. Bows, crossbows, laser rifles, dirks, slings. Even the children had fought. But the attacking force had been too strong. There was nothing living—except the sea birds—left in Tobermory.

"Well, then," said Diarmid calmly. "Not only am I a bad general, but I am now a general without troops."

"How could they have known?" demanded Rura.

Diarmid shrugged. "Others in Scotland knew that I had brought my people to Mull for temporary refuge. One of them must have been taken and persuaded to talk. It has happened before. I am a fool to have let my people stay in one place so long. But we needed the rest, and I thought—I thought—" He covered his face with his hands. "I killed them with my stupidity. I have not thought too clearly since Flora and Ewan died. I am a fool."

Rura attempted to comfort him. "You must not blame yourself. We live in an age of stupidity. We are all—"

"Who else is there to blame?" he shouted. "Who else but the man who presumes to command?"

"It could have been an accident. A routine patrol could have—"

"This was no routine patrol. Look at the wrecked gefcars, woman. Look at the bodies. Look at the damage. There must have been half a squadron, at least. And they knew exactly where to come."

"Well," said Rura softly, "it is over now. We cannot make it unhappen, and you must not exhaust yourself with guilt and grief. There are only the two of us, and night is coming down. What shall we do?"

Diarmid pulled himself together. "If you have the stomach for it, we must look at the dead. The weapons that are worth having, we must take. The clothes that are worth having, we must take. There are people in the Highlands who badly need both."

Rura was unnerved. "There isn't time," she pleaded. "It will be dark soon. We ought to get away. The Borderers may return."

Diarmid laughed grimly. "Madam exterminator, you do not know the ways of your own comrades. The Border Regiment never fights by night. Never. Darkness is the great equalizer. A bow is as good as a laser rifle in the dark. A dirk is better than both."

"I am not an exterminator!" she flared.

"So you are not. Then I must teach you to become one. I must teach you to exterminate the hellbitches in black. Well, then. So you cannot face the dead. Find us a cottage, Rura. Find us some food and fuel. Make us a fire, then we can hold each other and go to sleep as you wished. If there are nightmares, we will drown them in orgasm. I doubt that we could drown them in whiskey. There is not enough whiskey in the whole of Scotland to wash away this day's work. I will attend the dead."

"You hate me?" asked Rura.

"I hate myself. And you have become part of myself. Is that an answer?"

"It is the one I must accept."

Rura found a cottage that was relatively untouched. She gathered wood and made a fire. She found venison and even a little stale bread and some rancid butter. And in one half-burned cottage she found a small flask of whiskey. She did the best she could.

When Diarmid returned from his grisly task, there was

warmth and hot food awaiting him. He wolfed the food as if he had not eaten for days.

"I am an old man," he said, looking at her in the fire-light. "I am thirty-seven and probably one of the oldest men in Scotland."

"I love you," said Rura.

"Then you, too, are a fool. The clock ticks loud. It is unlikely that either of us will see another summer."

"All the more reason that we should enjoy this one," she said simply. "One summer is more than most people can expect in a lifetime."

XXII

It BEGAN to rain during the night. Diarmid, despite his misery and unhealed wounds, managed to sleep for quite long periods. Rura was tired, but she could not sleep. She could not sleep because the events of the past few days had turned all her attitudes upside down, had made her a stranger to herself. Surely it was not Rura Alexandra who had accepted male love joyfully, who had opened herself to a man while steam and smoke still rose from the dead lying nearby, while flies crawled over the vacant eyes of Borderers, while betrayal hung invisibly in the sad summer air?

No, it was not Rura Alexandra. It was some alien thing, some demonic creature of possession. But could one believe in demonic possession in this age of reason? Please, please, will the real Rura Alexandra come out and be recognized?

Perhaps there was no real Rura Alexandra. Perhaps there was only an animal with aching breasts and a will to live, whatever the cost.

She looked at Diarmid's face as he slept. A rough, weather-beaten face, almost coarse. Long hair, badly trimmed beard. A forehead full of lines. The face of an old man superimposed on the face of a child. No. Just the face of an ancient child.

She could still kill him and go back with honor. There would be no one to bear witness against her. She could go back, resign from the Border Regiment, return to a civilized' life, surrounded by beautiful women. She could rejoice again in the security of comfortable beds, sophisticated conversation, civilized love, elegant food.

Except that there would be memories, fragments of a savage beauty, crude echoes of passion.

Diarmid groaned in his sleep. His arm twitched. She looked at the stitches she had sewn in living flesh. There was no going back. There was only the completion of inevitable tragedy.

What kind of woman was Flora MacDiarmid? Had she, too, lain awake at night, counting the hours, wondering at the terrible persistence of this dinosaur who was a man?

There were too many questions, and no answers at all. Rura dozed a little before daybreak. The fire died. The rain stopped. The world seemed full of a great stillness.

Diarmid woke, stretched, groaned at the stiffness in his body, the pain in his arm. He touched Rura's breasts, stroked them, caressed them, made life surge through her flesh, destroyed all the whispering torments of the night.

"Romeo and Juliet," he said. "Once I had a book of Shakespeare. My father's. He never had time to teach me to read, but he would read the words to me. There was this play about two children who loved each other long ago. Their families were at war, or as near to being at war as makes no difference. Anyway, Romeo and Juliet had a rough time, and in the end they died, and their families decided it was pretty damn stupid to go on fighting."

"I know the play," said Rura. "Our families won't stop fighting—not until one of them is beaten."

Diarmid smiled. "Nor are we two children. This morning I feel a hundred years old. My people are lying dead out there, so are some of yours. And the killing will go on. None of us can stop it. Not even Curie Milford, who sits comfortably in London and stirs a female rabble with empty words. I am afraid."

"You, afraid?"

He gave a bitter laugh. "Did you not think it was possible, lassie? Somebody long dead once said that courage is an implacable treasure. You can spend it, but you can't put any back. I think I have spent a fair amount in my time. And now I am afraid."

Rura kissed him. "There is no shame in being afraid, Diarmid."

"You are missing the point, love. My people died yesterday. But I have options. I can set about raising another fighting force, or I can offer my services to another laird. Also, I have a gefcar, a trained pilot and more weapons at my disposal than I have ever had before. Diarmid MacDiarmid can still be a force to strike a certain chill in the hearts of those who draw their rations in Carlisle. But I am afraid. I am afraid to make decisions. Fear weakens my effectiveness. You understand?"

"I understand that recently you have endured much. You have wounds and you are tired."

Diarmid gripped her breast, hard. "You are still missing the point, Rura. I have lost so much, and all I have left to lose is you."

His fingers were hurting her, but she tried to ignore

the pain. "You are all I have left, also. I have learned to think of myself as a traitor. Is that not as hard as you learning to think of yourself as a coward?"

His grip relaxed. "So. We understand each other. The price for a few hours of peace on a small island was greater than I thought. I'm tired, Rura. I need to recover myself."

"You shall do that. I will look after you." She laughed. "It is my duty. I have been told that I am your woman."

"Do you believe it?"

"Are you my man?"

"A question for a question. Yes, I am your man."

"Then I must believe it."

"Well, Rura, listen to my appreciation of the situation, militarily and psychologically. We have here one demoralized ex-commander of guerillas and one renegade exterminator. We are in high summer, but autumn is days away, and the snows of winter are nearer than you think. Problem one: to survive. Problem two: to regain efficiency. I invite suggestions."

"May a renegade exterminator suggest that time is needed to regain efficiency? I know little about the Scottish winter; but I have heard that it can be very severe. I would suggest that the ex-commander of guerillas and the renegade exterminator find some secure retreat where they can survive the winter and regain efficiency by spring."

"The suggestion is noted. Also, it is a good one. At the moment, I am worth very little, and when winter comes, none of us in the Highlands are worth much. We have little energy for fighting. We are too busy trying to stay alive. The Borderers know this. Their mobility is affected, too; but nothing like ours. On clear days, they carry out long sweeps, looking for our smoke, or looking for hunters against the snow. So, Rura, we shall have to stay north of the Great Glen, if we are to have any chance of survival."

"The Great Glen?"

"Glen More. It runs northeast from sea to sea across the Highlands, from Fort William to the ruins of Inverness. Even the Borderers don't care to venture north of the Great Glen in winter. The blizzards would take out too many of their gefcars."

"You make the winter seem very frightening."

"It is frightening. It kills more of us than the exterminators do."

"But now it is still summer," said Rura, "and there is plenty of time to heal your arm and look for somewhere to live."

Diarmid went to the door of the cottage and opened it. "Ay, it's still summer. But I can smell the autumn. Cook us some breakfast. Use as much food as you want. There is more than we can carry from Mull, and my people are no longer hungry. I'm going to load the gefcar with everything we can possibly use and carry. The sooner we are away from this sad island, the better."

Rura came and stood at the door with him for a few moments. To the right, she knew, was the wreckage of machines and people. She did not look to the right. She looked only towards the beach and the sea. There was an onshore breeze. She breathed deeply, trying to inhale cleanness and peace. Then she went back into the cottage to prepare breakfast.

She knew that she would have to look at all that destruction again before she left Mull; pass among the bodies of men, women, children and exterminators; dis-

turb the flies, rats and birds in their enjoyment of an un-
expected harvest. But she forced herself not to think
about it.

The important thing was to prepare breakfast, and
then to take Diarmid out of this futile struggle for a
while. It would be something to have a winter without
fear and bloodshed. Even a Scottish winter.

Obediently, she cooked a large breakfast. There were
oats for porridge, and there were various wild birds' eggs,
and powdered milk, and a little salt. In Rura's gefcar
there were also standard rations and emergency rations;
but she did not want to go out to the gefcar. Not yet.

So she made salted porridge and a kind of scrambled
egg, and she found some hard, dry biscuits to give a little
body to the meal. When Diarmid returned, he ate rav-
enously, as if he had not eaten for a long time.

Rura was not hungry.

XXIII

IT WAS several days before they found the kind of refuge that would suit Diarmid. Rura had thought it would just be a simple matter of finding some derelict cottage fifty kilometers or more north of the Great Glen of Scotland. But Diarmid instructed her in the facts of life.

The house would have to be made of stone and capable, at least, of withstanding a surprise attack by a single gefcar patrol. It would have to be in wooded country so that it would be difficult to spot from the air and difficult for a gefcar to approach, and so that wood could be cut for fuel. It would have to be near fresh water and the sea for fishing. It would have to be near to deer forests and grouse moors for hunting. As well as being all of these things, it would have to be compact and comfortable, so that two people could sit out the Scottish winter without freezing or going crazy.

In short, it would have to be a paragon of a house.

Surprisingly, they found it. They found it after searching almost the entire seaward side of the Northwest Highlands. The search tired Rura, and hardened her and gave her some idea of the kind of life that Diarmid had led since he had been born. At nights, they slept in tattered sleeping bags under a much-patched tent that was neither rainproof nor windproof. They no longer lived by the clock, they lived by the sun and the stars. When the sun went down it was time to sleep. When daybreak came, it was time to wake. It was Diarmid's custom to hunt at first light. He would go out of the tent, taking a crossbow and bolts, leaving Rura drugged with sleep, aching with discomfort. Sometimes he would bring back a hare or a grouse. Once he returned with a young red deer slung over his shoulders. He taught Rura to pluck and clean birds, to gut animals and fish. At first she found the work revolting. Later, it seemed quite natural. Once, when she was filthy from gutting trout by the side of a stream, Diarmid took her and made love to her. The entrails of the fish were still in her hands, there was dew on the grass, and she was cold, dispirited and hungry. But Diarmid lay between her legs and she heard the murmurings of the stream, and looked past his head at the cloud patterns in the sky. And time froze, and the experience was locked in the crystal of memory for ever.

And, one day, they found the house. It was a wonderful house, a rare house. No one had plundered it. It must have endured, collecting dust and mildew, for a hundred years. There were two skeletons in it. One lay on a bed, a woman, judging by the tattered clothes. One lay sprawled across a table, a man. There was an antique handgun on the table, rusted, useless, with four unused bullets welded by time into its chamber. There were rats also. Rats, spiders, beetles.

The house was near the dead fishing village of Applecross. It stood in a small clearing in a small forest. Not far away was a stream. Not far away was the sea, and not for beyond that was the island of Skye.

The house was tough, squat, sturdy. Gray stone walls,

gray slate roof. The windows were small but several still had their original glass. The door was locked and bolted. Diarmid had to batter his way in. There were scutterings in the semidarkness. Rura drew back, afraid.

Diarmid grinned. "There are candles and lamps in the gefcar," he said. "Let us have light in here. And I will build a fire and drive the wild life away. There's nothing to be afraid of, love. The only things you have to fear in the Highlands are the weather and the women in black."

Presently, with lamplight illuminating dark corners, and with a wood fire dispersing the dampness of the decades, the house seemed almost cheerful, except for the two sad skeletons in the bedroom.

"I wonder what kind of people they were," said Rura. She had got over her initial shock. Dry bones were less terrible, less real, then recently dead bodies.

Diarmid studied them. "Despairing people in a despairing world. Maybe we'll find out their names. Little good it will do us or them. By the look of it, he shot her and then himself. Maybe they were ill, maybe they were starving, maybe they had seen something of the way the hellbitches work. . . . I'm going to take the bones outside. If you have no stomach for it, go and sort out the things we will need tonight from the gefcar."

"Will you . . . will you bury them?"

"Do you want me to?"

"Yes . . . yes, I think I'd like it. I'm stupid, Diarmid, and I know nothing can hurt them now. But I would like to think of them as being at rest together."

Diarmid held her for a moment. "You are stupid, Rura. But mankind needs a little stupidity. I can't bury them today. There is too much to do. But tomorrow I'll dig them a little grave in the forest. They won't need much. And you shall give them flowers in return for the home they have given us."

When Diarmid touched the bones, they fell apart. Rura went out so that he should not see her tears. In the end, he had to get a shawl to hold the bones. It was obviously the woman's shawl, damp, easily torn, almost colorless now, and with holes in it where rats or other creatures had worked. But it was something personal, and therefore fitting. He laid the bones in it very carefully, drew the ends together, knotted them, and took the light bundle out into the forest. He laid it under a tall pine tree. They would only need a very small grave. Smaller than he would have thought.

Meanwhile, Rura had begun the work of translating a mausoleum into a home. First she brought in weapons, then food, then clothing, then blankets. Such, she reflected sadly, was the order of priority. Presently there was time to properly explore the house, though it was not large enough to warrant extensive exploration.

The accommodation was all at ground level. One bedroom, one living room, one kitchen, one bathroom. But there was a cellar. In the center of the living room there was a trap door. The cellar was amazingly dry. It had been used as a storeroom for logs and unwanted possessions. Probably also for food.

There was a trunk in the cellar, a steel trunk, locked. Diarmid broke the lock. Inside the trunk were the remains of a white dress, an old wedding dress perhaps, and a man's black suit. And underneath these were books. All kinds of books. A history of the Highland Clearances, a book on astronomy, the poems of Robert

Burns, the novels of Sir Walter Scott. Books, books, books.

Rura gazed at them in amazement. Diarmid gazed at them wistfully.

"When the snows come and the evenings are long," he said, "you will teach me to read?"

"My love, I will teach you to read."

Diarmid laughed. "Who knows, if it is a long winter I may have time to turn into an intellectual. I wanted Ewan to read. While he was alive, I was at times foolishly optimistic. I thought it still might be possible to fight our way to some kind of agreement, some kind of peace, which would allow men to educate themselves and stop living as savages."

"Is that no longer possible?"

"Rura, face facts. The deaths of those you love is a great stimulant for facing facts. Wales is all but pacified, each year drastically reduces our numbers in the Highlands, the Republic of Anglia grows stronger. Time is on the side of Curie Milford's female robots. Your people can clone and use parthenogenesis."

"They are not my people!"

"So. I am sorry. The women in the south, then. They can increase their numbers at will by means of sciences and skills that I do not fully understand. We can only increase by getting our women with child. And we do not have many women. What is happening in the rest of the world, I know not. But here, in the land where I live, the clock ticks loud."

Rura sighed. "I must get some food ready. Tomorrow we will make this house into *our* home."

"You must also check the fuel in the gefcar before I cover it with branches and bracken. We have used it sparingly these last few days, but I think there cannot be many kilometers left in it."

Rura went outside with him and read the fuel gauge. There was, perhaps, enough fuel left for about a hundred kilometers at moderate speed, medium lift, or sixty kilometers flat out.

"How will it survive the winter?" asked Diarmid. I know little of these things."

"Well enough. They are designed to withstand extremes of climate."

"Praise be to female engineers. When spring comes, if we live that long, we shall be able to travel in comfort to our destruction."

Rura turned and looked at the house in the forest. The air was warm and it was still high summer, though the subtle promise of autumn was beginning to reveal itself. She was not concerned with the problems of next spring, nor even the problems of winter. She was content simply to accept each day as it came. Each day was a bonus. A treasure stolen from eternity.

XXIV

THE SHORTENING days followed each other rapidly. Long grasses shed their seeds, turned yellow, became flattened by rain. The air was sharp, the nights cool. Sere leaves fell from beech, oak, ash. The evergreens preserved their illusion of immortality.

The house became a home. Its previous occupants lay tranquilly under a meter of Scottish earth, their presence indicated only by a wooden marker that was already collecting lichen. They had been called Jenny and Duncan Lindsay. Rura had found a few barely decipherable letters in the trunk—letters that, as their contents indicated, had been delivered by the only postal service available in Scotland, the traveling men. Men with dirks and bows who had risked their lives to maintain some kind of communication between the dwindling fighting clans. Jenny had been originally of the Murray clan. Duncan Lindsay had taken a fancy to her and had painstakingly written out a simple contract of marriage in block capitals.

It read: "I, Duncan Lindsay, free man of Scotland, take Jenny Murray, free woman of Scotland, to wife. This marriage is binding unto death, which, by the grace of God, is close at all times. Signed: Duncan Lindsay."

To which Jenny had added: "I, Jenny Murray, of my free will accept Duncan Lindsay in marriage. My issue shall be his issue only. This I swear. Signed: Jenny Murray, now by this act become Jenny Lindsay."

The paper was torn, brittle, stained. The penciled writing was barely legible. To Rura, the words were the most beautiful she had ever read. The document was the most wonderful thing she had ever possessed.

She read it to Diarmid one evening by candlelight. He held her close and said, "When I have learned to write a fair hand, I, too, will make such a statement, and you will put your name to it. Who knows, a hundred years from now, someone will find the paper and be moved to wonder."

"Or moved to tears," said Rura.

He shook his head. "The women of the future will not weep for us. More likely, they will laugh."

"Unless they realize what they have lost."

Diarmid gave a grim laugh. "What they have not known, they cannot miss. In a world without men, they will need to remember us as something evil. How else could they retain their pride, their self-respect?"

Rura had no answer, except to hold him close.

One morning there was a frost upon the ground. It was the morning that Rura was sick.

She had breakfasted on blackberries and apple, on delicious fresh trout, on new bread baked from the dwindling supply of flour. It was a wonderful breakfast. There was no reason for her to be sick. And yet she rushed out of the house and watched her breakfast fall, steaming, on the frosty grass.

Diarmid stroked her back and comforted her. She did

not know what had happened. He did. He had seen it before.

"So you are with child, Rura. Isn't that something?"

She was amazed, horrified. And yet she knew that she should not have been greatly surprised.

"This is pregnancy?"

"This is pregnancy."

She began to shiver and tremble. "What shall I do? What shall I do?"

"You will endure it, woman. Better than you have endured it." Diarmid wiped the vomit away and kissed her. "Perhaps it will be a son. If I knew what the date was, I would set it down. A date to remember. But all I can say is, early in the autumn I knew that my woman was with child."

A terrible thought struck Rura. "It may not be your child, Diarmid. That day on Loch Lomond. Your men—" She did not really want to think about what had happened that day.

"So. It is a possibility. It does not matter. The child will be mine. I shall shape it. If I live, if you live, I shall shape it."

"How do you know I am pregnant?"

"Your breasts are larger, your belly swells, you are sick. You are pregnant."

She was terrified and full of joy. She was humiliated and full of pride. It was all very strange.

"Is there anything I have to do, or not do? Is there anything I have to learn? Forgive me. It is confusing."

"They trained you to kill," said Diarmid drily, "not to give birth. A splendid irony. Don't worry, lass. I have delivered before. I can do it again."

She was not troubled too much by the morning sickness. After about ten days, it virtually disappeared, returning only rarely.

Rura found a name for the house because, as she said, it was the kind of house that deserved a name. She called it Lindsays' Haven, to commemorate the two who lay buried in the forest. She kept the little grave tidy, found late flowers to put upon it. Sometimes she went down to the sea—just far enough away for a pleasant walk—and brought back great scallop shells for an ornamental border. And she began to build a cairn out of attractive-looking pebbles. She was determined to give Jenny and Duncan something for Lindsays' Haven. She got a sharp piece of flint and spent one whole morning scratching the name in large, bold letters on the great slab of stone above the doorway. Diarmid watched her, amused. He thought she was like a child—a child with a woman's body. He marveled at the change that pregnancy had brought. She seemed both younger and older at the same time.

Diarmid spent his days hunting, fishing, looking for fruit and cutting fuel for winter. Peat and dried wood were in abundance. Provided one accepted the risk of letting smoke drift up into the sky at night, there need be little danger of freezing in the winter. It was an acceptable risk. He had never known the Borderers come so far north in the Highlands late in the year. Besides, there was always the gefcar. He had hidden it away, under piles of bracken and light branches of spruce about four hundred meters from the house, making sure that it had a fairly clear avenue out of the forest. Rura had said that there was only about a hundred kilometers of running left in it; but that would surely be enough for an emergency. She had taught him how to start the engines and manipulate the controls. He was sure he could handle it if he had to.

Rura spent her days learning to forget that she had ever been an exterminator, learning to become a woman. It was an exciting process. It was as if she were peeling away a superficial persona and discovering something quite different underneath. She taught herself to sew, and made clothes for Diarmid and herself out of the old clothes and pieces of material that they had managed to bring from Mull. She learned how to cook venison, fish, game birds and beef from wild Highland cattle in a variety of ways. She learned how to make use of the salt in seawater. She learned how to obtain and preserve animal fats and oils. She learned how to stretch skins and make them supple, what to do with the pelts of rabbits and sheep. She learned how to preserve apple rings for the winter, to recognize and collect edible fungus, leaves and berries. She learned to sing the old songs that Diarmid loved, to do the things that would please him; she learned when to be passive and when to take the initiative, and how to respond to excite him. She began to feel proud of her swollen breasts and swollen belly. These were the outward and visible signs of the true nature of womanhood.

In the evenings, as she had promised, she taught Diarmid to read. He learned to recognize letters quickly. He learned to recognize the shorter words quickly.

"My love is like a red, red rose. . . ."

He already knew the ancient song. But when he saw the words of the poem on paper that was brittle and flecked with brown spots, an explosion of understanding happened in his mind.

"And I will come again, my love, though t'were ten thousand mile."

Soon he was reading the novels of Sir Walter Scott aloud by candlelight, while logs crackled on the hearth and showers of sparks went up the chimney to scatter and die in the autumn night.

The trunk that had belonged to Jenny and Duncan Lindsay contained treasures beyond his imagining. The book on astronomy knocked him sideways. The stars had always been just things that were there in a clear sky, soft in summer, diamond-hard in the cold clarity of winter.

He discovered, with profound shock, that they were suns like the sun that warmed earth. He learned about stellar distances. He learned about light-years and came to realize that, depending upon perspective, Earth and the problems of mankind could seem very small indeed.

Autumn came early in the Highlands, an unusually dry autumn for Scotland, cold and frosty at night, abnormally warm and sunny during the day. Indian summer. Diarmid knew that this kind of weather was called Indian summer; but he did not know why.

At times, he felt guilty that he was not busy raising another fighting force or offering his services to another commander. But it was too late in the year for such projects. The Scottish winter gave little scope for offensive action. Normally, the Border Regiment was content with routine local patrols. Normally, the Highlanders were content to survive, if they could. The Scottish winter was worth another Border Regiment to Curie Milford.

The deceptive Indian summer fascinated Rura. She loved to be able to walk by day in the forest, watching the rich gold shafts of sunlight penetrate almost magically the green umbrellas of the trees. She loved also to be able to stroll along the seashore—the sea was no more than three kilometers from the house—looking for stranded crabs at low tide, collecting shells, watching the western sunlight play upon the desolate isles of Rona, Raasay and Skye.

But most of all, she loved the evenings when a log fire crackled on the hearth, when the stewpot simmered, redolent of meat and herbs and mushrooms, and Diarmid was home from the hills. This was a way of life that was hundreds of years old, she knew. A simple life. A life compounded of hunting and survival and warmth and love. On such evenings, when the reading and the singing was done, she and Diarmid would tell each other of their early lives, seeking to understand each other, greedy for knowledge of each other's background, trying hard to bring alien worlds together.

Rura was the parthenogenetic child of Aimée Alexandra, surgeon of distinction, herself a parthenogenetic child. Aimée Alexandra had specialized in heart-lung transplants. She had extended the useful lives of dozens of women of the Republic of Anglia. She had even given a new heart to Curie Milford. Then, unaccountably, she had committed suicide.

It had happened when Rura was sixteen and already a distinguished resident student in the Greer College of Emancipation. Aimée, ironically, had lasered her own heart. No one knew why. The official explanation was depression due to overwork. Because she had devised the Alexandra Rejection Treatment, she was given a state funeral. Rura, who, after the age of ten, had seen very little of her mother, became a ward of the Republic.

Diarmid MacDiarmid was the son of Diarmid Mac-

Diarmid, a Highland chieftain who simply could not comprehend what had happened in the south. The Republic of Anglia, established long before his birth, was inexplicable. A parcel of women playing silly games, that was all it was. He gathered his clan and marched towards Anglia, secure in the belief that those damnable women would evaporate before a determined fighting force. He was defeated and destroyed at Edinburgh. His force of three hundred Highlanders was annihilated by twenty Borderers. The Borderers had gefcars and laser weapons. Diarmid MacDiarmid's force did not. The young Diarmid had been left with his mother. He was eight years old at the time.

Rura found it easy to understand the kind of life that Diarmid had led. She was getting a taste of it herself. Diarmid, on the other hand, found it difficult to envisage the kind of world that Rura had deserted. He knew about exterminators and the use of weapons and tactical warfare. But the only cities he had ever seen were dead cities, where one scavenged for metal, glass, fabrics, utensils, tools, weapons.

A city such as London defeated his imagination. He who had spent his life in the wild, empty stretches of the Highlands, could not comprehend how a million people —a million women—could live together in harmony and in such proximity. The claustrophobia of city life would have driven him mad. He could understand the vast distances between the stars better than he could understand how human beings, even women, could consent to live— as it seemed to him—literally piled on top of each other in high-rise blocks that seemed like cages not fit even for rats.

But though his experience was limited, his perception

was not. The one thing he believed—and believed with a ferocious intensity—was that women could not properly be human without men. It was a belief to which Rura was already more than half converted. She no longer thought of men as pigs, as creatures whose sole aim was to subjugate and humiliate women, inhibiting their creative urges, making them feel inferior.

Life with Diarmid had made her feel proud. Someone needed her both as a sex object and as a person. Someone needed her enough to risk his life for her. Someone needed her vagina, her womb, her breasts and her spirit. Someone needed her to the death.

Rura had been loved by women, but not like that. She had never known such intense, exhausting demands. Nor had she ever known such fulfilment.

It opened her eyes. No woman had ever needed her as Diarmid needed her. Nor had she needed any woman as she had needed Diarmid.

As the Scottish autumn deepened towards winter, as her belly swelled and the tightness grew in her breasts, Rura learned that happiness was a very simple thing. It consisted of being one's self.

She knew also that she lived in a world where such happiness could not last.

Rura Alexandra, onetime exterminator, had a simple ambition now. She wanted only to live long enough to bear her child—not a clone child, not a parthenogenetic child, but one sired by man in anger or in love—and see it on the road to maturity.

Such a small ambition, really.

But, perhaps, too great to be fulfilled.

XXV

EARLY ONE morning snow came. A light dusting, the visiting card of winter. Soon there would be more snow. Soon winter would come to stay. Rura knew that the months ahead would be long and hard, that food would be scarce and that Lindsays' Haven would be locked in an icy and lonely grip. She did not care. She had Diarmid and she had the child in her belly. She did not care. Somehow, Diarmid would find the food. Somehow, they would survive the winter. And in the spring the baby would be born.

She could not be sure that the baby's father was Diarmid. She could only be sure that its father was a man, and that would have to be enough. She found herself remembering the ex-captain of the Welsh Guard, that old weatherbeaten woman who had appeared one morning, long ago in another universe, by the edge of the Serpentine. Rura felt sorry for her, desperately sorry. She was beginning to understand something of what the woman felt about the child that had begun to grow inside her. She would have liked to go back in time and kiss the old woman and weep for her abortion, and promise her that somehow the race of man would survive.

She could feel it in her own belly. Well, it was something to believe. It was something one needed to believe. . . .

The snow transformed the forest into a wonderland. Tiny snow crystals edged the trees with cold fire and transformed pine needles into delicate ornaments. Rura walked among the trees, enchanted, listening to the silence and the stillness. Diarmid was out hunting the red deer. Not with laser weapons, of which there were plenty, but with a crossbow. He said it was cleaner.

In the evening he would come home with or without venison, it did not matter. Not yet. Food was not yet a problem. In the evening he would come home and there would be the intimacy of firelight and touch. Of such was the kingdom of heaven.

Rura walked through the forest, a laser rifle in her hand, marveling at the clean, cold beauty of the snow. Diarmid had taught her never to go out without a weapon, never to be in any situation where a weapon was not in easy reach. But strolling in the quiet forest, with not a breath of wind to disturb the snow, she hated the laser rifle, symbol of destruction, and found it hard to believe that she lived in a world where one set of human beings was dedicated to the extermination of another.

She looked back at her footprints in the snow and was suddenly conscious that all things were transient. Tonight or tomorrow, perhaps, the snow would melt or more snow would fall; and the footprints would disappear for ever. So it was with people, unless—unless they could create something that would outlive them, and, in its turn, bring forth life.

Suddenly, there was a noise ahead. She turned with a start, her hand automatically tightening on the rifle. Not thirty meters away, framed by two pine trees, stood a huge red deer. A stag, with the characteristic heavy neck and the great antlers. A magnificent beast. He had been nibbling grass, evidently, that poked in tufts through the snow. But now he stared at Rura calmly, almost conspiratorially.

She looked at his eyes—large, brown expressive eyes, without fear. She thought of Diarmid, out hunting the red deer. What would he not give to be where she stood —with the crossbow in his hand, and a bolt ready.

Rura had seen many deer in the Highlands; but this one was surely the largest of them all. Larger than life. A superb specimen. There must be more than a hundred kilos of good venison on him.

She was conscious of the rifle in her hand. It would be so easy to kill. She ought to kill. She and Diarmid had not eaten venison for days. Diarmid would be proud of her if she brought down a deer like that. They could feast as much as they wished and still have enough venison left over to dry off into long thin strips to be salted away against the time when the hunting was bad.

She raised the rifle slowly. The stag did not move. She raised the rifle and sighted it. But then she saw the look in the stag's eyes. Not fear, it seemed, but a question. A silent question.

Strange. She could only be imagining it. She held the rifle steady; but she could not kill. She tried to think of venison roasting; but she could not associate the juicy, imaginary cuts of meat with this magnificent creature.

Slowly, she lowered the rifle. She and the stag still gazed at each other. There did not seem now to be a question in the creature's eyes. Only a look that seemed to indicate a kind of mutual understanding.

151

She became aware of a faint noise in the sky. A familiar noise. A growing noise. The stag shook its head, as if emerging from a trance. Then it bounded away, its hooves drumming dully on the ground, kicking up fine showers of snow. It was out of sight in seconds.

Rura gave a deep sigh. The enchanted moments had been shattered by the rhythmic noises of reality.

She looked up through the trees and saw the chopper cruising slowly at an altitude of about five hundred meters. What was a chopper doing this far north at this time of the year? Was it spotting for a string of gefcars? Were the hellbitches disregarding habit and prudence to carry their war to the northwest Highlands, even in winter?

Suddenly she was dreadfully afraid. Not for herself, for Diarmid. Rura had the cover of the forest. She hoped desperately that Diarmid was not exposed on open ground. She knew just how he would look from an altitude of five hundred meters. A strange, untidy insect, scrambling with painful slowness over the bleak white landscape.

The snow was no longer a crystalline miracle. It was an enemy. A traitor, exposing the pursued to the pursuers. . . . He would be such an easy target from the chopper. No need to whistle up the gefcars. He couldn't go into the heather—only crouch on the snow and try to exchange an arrow for a laser beam. They would come down low for him, with laughter on their lips.

Rura was shaking, impotently shaking with fear. She tried to discipline herself, to stop herself from thinking. She must not go to pieces.

Then she remembered something else. The remains of last night's fire still smoldered on the hearth at Lindsays'

Haven. Diarmid had told her to put it out before she left the house. But the morning had been chilly; and there was so little smoke from the embers that she had been tempted to let them burn themselves out, so that home would be just a little warm when she returned.

But even a thin wisp of smoke would rise up like a signpost on this still, bright morning.

Oh, stupid sow! Oh, brainless bitch! Rura cursed herself futilely.

The chopper was circling and losing height. Had it seen something? What had it seen?

Please, goddess, then let it come really low! Let me get but one clear sweep at it! Damn these trees! Damn this bloody forest. I can't see the chopper, now. I can't see it.

But she could hear it circling. It circled twice, came back briefly into view twice. But not within laser range. Rura wept with fear and frustration.

As the sound of the chopper's engines faded slowly towards the southeast, Rura began to run back to Lindsays' Haven. Twice she slipped and fell in the snow. The second time she twisted her ankle. *If I go on like this,* she thought, despising herself and her vulnerability, *I'll lose the baby.*

That sobered her. That made her collect her wits together and begin to think clearly.

As the house came into view, she saw that there was indeed a thin skein of smoke rising from its chimney, a plume of white wood smoke wavering in the still air. Her spirits fell. Surely the chopper must have seen it—if it were looking for such things. And it would be, unless. . . . Mentally, Rura put herself in a chopper and looked down on Lindsays' Haven. White smoke against white snow. Would she see it? Answer: no. But that was the answer she wanted. . . .

Where had the chopper been circling? It didn't look as if it had been circling the house. It had looked as if it had been circling a patch of forest nearer to the sea, nearer to where she had stood. But why would it do that?

The gefcar! Maybe the camouflage over the gefcar was not as good as Diarmid had thought. Rura hurried through the forest to see. The camouflage was fine. The snow had helped. No, the chopper could not have found the gefcar. Maybe it had just been taking a look at some deer. That would be a nice thing to believe. A comfortable thing.

Rura made her way slowly back to Lindsays' Haven, depressed. Diarmid must have seen or heard the chopper also. If he had, he would probably decree that they leave the area and find somewhere else to live. If he knew that the chopper had been circling over the forest, he would certainly decide to leave. For him, choppers meant only one thing.

Rura did not want to leave Lindsays' Haven. It was the first true home she had ever known. It was the place where she had known much love. It was the place where her belly and her breasts had grown plump and proud. It was the home that had been bequeathed to her and Diarmid by dead lovers. . . .

No other place, no other house, could ever mean the same. For here she had truly known what it was to be a woman.

She went into the house, flung her laser rifle down and sat staring at the embers on the hearth. She did not want to move again. She wanted her baby to be born here. She wanted Lindsays' Haven to reach fulfillment.

She made a deal with herself—a pact with a female devil. If Diarmid had seen the helicopter, she would tell him what had happened. And she would accept the consequences.

But if Diarmid had not seen the chopper, then there was no real cause to worry him unduly. It could have been circling because the pilot felt like circling. It could have been circling because this was the most northerly point of the patrol, and it was about to turn back. It could also have been circling because of smoke rising from the chimney of a derelict house.

Diarmid did not return until dusk. He had managed to kill a very young, very small deer. He dropped it on the floor with an air of achievement.

"How went the day, love?"

"Well enough. I walked in the forest and spent much time thinking how lucky I was."

He kissed her. "I stalked this bloody animal for about ten kilometers. A most perverse creature. It moved in a great circle. When I finally had the chance of a decent shot, it was little more than a kilometer from home. One bolt was needed, that was all."

Rura thought of the magnificent stag she had seen. Diarmid's kill was a pygmy by comparison.

"It is a fine deer," she said.

He laughed. "You do it much honor. This morning I saw a stag that would have made four of him. I was near the sea, with the sound of the waves rattling in my ears. Otherwise I would have heard him coming. He passed well within range, too. Let us get a fire up, lass. It will be a cold night again, by the feel of it."

Perhaps the stag that Diarmid had seen was the wonderful creature that she had encountered in the forest.

Evidently Diarmid had not seen the chopper. Nor could he have heard it, probably for the same reason that he had not heard the stag.

So Rura said nothing. She relighted the fire, while Diarmid made sure that the covers at the windows would not let any light through. Then she began to cook the whiting and the large lobster that Diarmid had brought back from the sea the day before.

With darkness, the wind had begun to rise. The noise of it in the trees outside sounded like the sea. The fire was bright once more, with logs spitting and crackling, and flames leaping up the chimney, and warm shadows dancing in the room.

This cottage in the Highlands was a harsh contrast to the air-conditioned, centrally heated civilization that existed in the Republic of Anglia. It was a harsh wonderful contrast. It was a small, magic cosmos—a place where a man and a woman could fit together emotionally and physically and find their true selves.

Rura wanted to live at Lindsays' Haven all the days of her life.

XXVI

THE FOLLOWING morning, there was more snow. Not much, and such small, dry, powdery crystals; but enough to enhance the wintry image of the forest without making movement too difficult. Diarmid, convinced that winter was settling in early, hated the snow. To him it meant shortage of game, hunger. He had endured too many Scottish winters to be impressed by the antiseptic beauty of the forest, the bleak grandeur of the hills.

He cut the skin off the deer he had killed and sliced the venison carefully. Then he went out hunting once more. Much meat would have to be dried and sealed and packed in a snow cache if the winter were going to be as long as he thought. Biltong was simple to make, though the process was arduous: cutting the meat into strips as thin as possible, then hanging the strips to dry in the sun and the wind if the weather were right. If the weather were poor, a fire could be used for the drying, though some of the fire-dried meat would always go bad before it was properly dehydrated.

Rura went into the forest, ostensibly to collect fuel and twigs for kindling. But this was just an excuse to allow her to roam among the trees, exulting in their beauty, daydreaming.

She had developed a secret vice. She constructed imaginary utopias where people did not have to spend their lives trying to find enough food to survive or trying to kill each other. In her mind, she created a world where there was no war between women and men and where she could bear her child in peace and watch it grow up to take some creative part in the advancement of mankind.

It was pleasant to walk in the forest and dream dreams and collect wood. It was pleasant also to anticipate the intimacies of evening—food shared by firelight, books shared by firelight, love shared by firelight.

She returned to Lindsays' Haven with enough wood and kindling to last for one and a half fires. That was her customary target—to keep a little ahead, against the days of storm and illness. Against the time when the snow would be too deep, when she would be too fat to venture out, when the elements would imprison her and Diarmid in their stone-walled bastion of paradise.

She was in a typical reverie when she reached the house. She had not forgotten yesterday's visitation by the chopper; but she had pushed it to the back of her mind. It was something she did not want to know about. It was an intrusion. Otherwise she might have noticed the footprints in the snow, leading to the door.

She walked into Lindsays' Haven, and saw the two hellbitches, the women in black, pointing laser rifles at her.

"Relax, sow. Otherwise, burn and be damned." The Borderer who spoke was very young. Golden-haired, blue-eyed. Excitement and anticipation showed in her face. She wanted to kill.

Rura dropped the wood she was holding and stood

motionless. She felt very sorry for the young exterminator. Then she felt angry. No one had the right to intrude in Lindsays' Haven.

"Stand facing the wall, sow," continued the young exterminator. "Hands over your head on the wall, feet apart. Try not to breathe. It makes us nervous."

Rura felt hands under her arms, feeling her waist, hips, even between her legs. Once the touch of a woman had been familiar, acceptable. Now it was alien.

"Turn round, pig meat."

While the other, the dark-haired exterminator, continued to cover her with the rifle, the young one felt her breasts and belly. She held each breast tightly for a moment, as if she would like to tear it off.

"So! One in the bag. Well, pig-breeder, the party is over."

The exterminator drew back, knotted her fist and slammed it into Rura's stomach. She fell to her knees, doubled up, moaning, gasping. The Borderer grabbed her hair, forced her head back, looked down with satisfaction at the pain on Rura's face.

"Where is he, sow?"

"I don't know."

The exterminator still held her hair. A foot came up and kicked her. Rura groaned, tried to block out the pain.

"Where is he?"

"Hunting . . . hunting somewhere."

The exterminator chuckled, and threw Rura full length on the floor by her hair.

"We'll wait. He'll be glad of visitors."

Rura lay on the floor, gasping, trying to cope with the pain, trying to think. Customarily, Diarmid would not return until shortly before dusk. That gave her time to do something. Just what, she did not yet know. But something.

The other exterminator spoke. Her voice was more gentle, perhaps because she was older. "Child, you don't have to die. If you help us, you don't have to die. We can rehabilitate you, maybe even let you bear your child. What is your name?"

That is something, thought Rura. *They don't know. They think I'm just another Highland woman. How could they know? I was at Carlisle such a short time.*

There was another kick. "Name!" demanded the one who enjoyed inflicting punishment.

"Jenny Lindsay."

A laugh. "This is no longer your haven, Jenny Lindsay. The pig, your man. What is his name?"

"Duncan."

Golden Hair talked to the older one. "Duncan Lindsay. Is he on the list, Garnet?"

"No, he's not on the list."

"Small fry! Just our luck. Not Ballantrae or Hamilton or MacDiarmid. Only some stupid little crofter who still thinks he lives in a man's world. Well, I suppose it's better than nothing. It's a head. Another head for the record before winter closes in." She turned to Rura. "Stand up, pig lover. When will he come back?"

"I don't know."

Golden Hair slapped her face. "Try to know. It's less tiring."

"I don't know."

Golden Hair was about to slap her again, but the other exterminator intervened. "That's enough, Willa. Call Carlisle, give our position, and tell them we have made a hit.

Tell them we'll call back when we decide to return or when we collect the pig."

Willa, seemed disappointed. She went out of the house, presumably to where the gefcar had been left.

The dark-haired exterminator stood up. "Well, Jenny Lindsay, it is a sad day for you."

"Yes," said Rura numbly.

"You are pretty. Despite the rags, you are pretty." She put the laser rifle down. "Have you ever seen a city full of people, Jenny?"

For a moment, Rura Alexandra, silver nipple, was tempted to laugh. But she remembered her role. "No. I'm just a poor Highland girl, trying to live in peace with her man."

"He will have to die, Jenny. That cannot be avoided. But you need not die, not if you have a friend."

"I have no friends."

Garnet came towards her. "You could have a friend. . . . If you were bathed, if you had fine clothes, you could look even prettier. Would you like that?"

"Yes," said Rura softly. "I would like that."

"With the right kind of friend, you might even keep your baby."

"I would like that very much," said Rura.

Garnet came close. She put her arms round Rura. "Kiss me. Then I will know, from the way you kiss, how much you would like to live."

Rura flinched, then concentrated on being Jenny Lindsay. Jenny, she thought, would have been greatly embarrassed by a woman's caress. Oddly, so now was Rura, who had kissed many women. "I have never kissed a woman," she said hesitantly, "not like that." She was wondering if she were still strong enough and agile

161

enough to deal with this exterminator and grab a rifle before the other one returned. She doubted it. There was a rhythmic pain in her stomach where she had been punched and kicked. But she would have to try. It was the only thing to do.

Garnet laughed. "Then now is the time to try it, little one. Don't you know that women are more passionate than men? They can love and love and love long after a man is spent."

She kissed Rura on the mouth, holding her close with one arm round her waist, fondling her. Rura tried to make some response, while surreptitiously moving her knee so that she could jerk it up into the exterminator's crotch.

She was not allowed to complete the movement. Garnet was too experienced for such tricks. The hand that had been fondling Rura delivered a short, vicious blow to her still aching stomach. Rura groaned and doubled up. As she went down, the Borderer swung at her head for good measure. It was slammed back against the edge of the table. Rura collapsed in a heap, unconscious for a moment or two, twitching. Then she was aware of pain once more. Pain in her head and body. She lay on the floor with her eyes closed, trying to get her breath, trying pitifully to think.

"For that," said the exterminator softly, "you have earned special treatment."

Rura heard footsteps and then the door close. The other one had returned.

"Carlisle advises that we don't stay north of the Grampians too long. They want us to call back every two hours. They ask if we need support. They are willing to send a chopper."

"Screw Carlisle. We don't need a chopper. If we lose the daylight we can stay here."

"What happened to baby?" The exterminator called Willa laughed. "She looks unhappy."

"She is unhappy. She tried to be clever. Get up, pig meat. That will teach you not to mix it with a real woman."

Rura got unsteadily to her feet, clutching her stomach, trying vainly to press the pain out of it.

"Back to square one, animal," said Willa. "When will the snout-faced one return?"

"I—I don't know."

The Borderer lifted her arm, as if to hit Rura again.

"At dusk. A little before dusk. That's when he usually —" Her voice trailed away.

"So. We wait. Baby will entertain us, won't you, baby?"

"I have an idea," said Garnet. She turned to Rura. "Make a fire, baby. Make a big fire. We will all be jolly and warm together."

"Willa smiled. "Lots of smoke. Yes, lots of smoke. With luck, he'll see it. With luck, the smoke will bring him."

Rura was beginning to recover her wits. A fire. Yes, a very big fire. The hellbitches thought it would bring Diarmid back. They were right. But it would also act as a warning. And Diarmid would know. He had lived long enough not to be fooled by a couple of hellbitches like these. He would know there was something wrong at Lindsays' Haven, and he would be ready to do something about it. That would be Rura's chance—when they knew Diarmid was near, and their attention was distracted for a few precious moments. There was a dirk on the mantelpiece, an iron poker on the hearth. With dirk or poker or even bare hands, there would be an opportunity to do something. There had to be.

So she filled the hearth with logs, watched the flames grow higher and begin to roar in the chimney, felt the heat of the fire bring sweat to her face and arms and shoulders. Or was it fear?

Outside there was a strange barking. Rura glanced through the window. There was nothing to be seen but the snow, and the trees and the cold sunlight.

The exterminators stood back from the window and door, their laser rifles ready.

"What is the noise, sow?" asked Garnet quietly.

The barking came again.

Rura kept her face expressionless. "Deer. Roe deer. Sometimes the males bark at each other."

But it was not deer barking. The sound was not quite harsh enough. It was Diarmid warning that he was close at hand.

"I can see nothing," said Garnet. "If you are being clever again, baby, I'll burn you. Deer, barking!" She snorted with contempt, but she did not entirely disbelieve.

There was more barking. It sounded nearer.

Willa went to the door, opened it cautiously and glanced outside. "I'm going to take a look around. Cover me."

"Be careful, Willa. That deer just may smell of pig." The exterminator turned to Rura. "Lie facedown on the floor, over there by the wall. Don't move. You'd be amazed how long it takes to die with the right kind of burn."

Rura went to the far wall and lay down obediently. If she were going to do anything, now was the time to do it. But the exterminator was by the window on the other side of the room. Before Rura could get to her, she would be cut in two. The poker. . . . That was still a possibility. But it was so far away. Rura began to inch towards it. She prayed for noise, for distraction. But, outside, there was now only silence. Inside there was only the crackling of the fire.

Garnet stood by the window, peering out. From the way she looked anxiously from side to side, Rura judged that the other Borderer was now out of view. She had managed to move about a meter nearer the hearth. Two more meters to go, and she would have the poker. The heat of the now roaring wood fire was intense. It hurt her eyes, but she continued to edge forward.

From outside there came a faint thwack, immediately followed by a terrible high-pitched scream that died into a gurgle. Then, briefly, there was silence. Then the barking started once more.

Garnet stepped back from the window, white-faced, shaken. She glanced at Rura, noting the stealthy movement. "Freeze, pig-breeder, or I'll roast the thing in your womb. So that was a roe deer! And I suppose we just heard Willa laughing with pleasure. Stand up, sow. Unless you do exactly as I tell you, I'll burn you so that you take a week to die."

Rura stood up. She managed to smile. "The wild deer can be vicious when provoked," she said evenly. "Especially the males."

Garnet gave a grim smile. "Then let us hunt deer. You will walk out through the doorway, baby. My rifle will be pointed at the small of your back. You will call this —this roe deer. You will tell him that unless he presents himself unarmed before a count of ten, you will burn.

165

And when I say burn, I mean burn. In this, I am an expert."

Rura laughed. There was a terrible anger in the way she laughed. And pride. "You think I will play it your way, hellbitch? Start burning. The man out there is Diarmid MacDiarmid. He went hunting with a crossbow. Now, I think, he may have a laser rifle. Burn me, and see what happens. I will not take long to die. You, on the other hand, will find that minutes can seem like hours, and hours like years."

The exterminator turned away from the window, astounded. "MacDiarmid! The man himself?"

"The man himself." Rura forgot her pain, forgot her fear. "One man who is worth a squadron of Borderers. You have hit the jackpot."

There was a sound of breaking glass. Garnet swung towards the window. As she did so, the door crashed open and Diarmid burst in, laser rifle in his hands. He registered it all in one split-second glance.

"Drop it, hellbitch! Don't move, don't breathe, don't speak."

Garnet froze, her rifle pointing the wrong way.

"Drop it!"

She dropped it. Diarmid allowed himself to smile at Rura.

"Take the lady's toy, my dear. We must remove temptation."

Rura picked up the rifle. "Diarmid, you are all right?"

"I am fine. And you?"

"I'm all right now."

XXVII

THE EXTERMINATOR had been trussed like an animal, her wrists tied to her ankles. She sat hunched on the floor, her knees under her chin. Diarmid regarded her almost benevolently.

"You are lucky," he said pleasantly. "You have already lived longer than most I have encountered. If your conversation is instructive, you may earn a quick death. Does the proposition interest you?"

Garnet said nothing. But she met his gaze, her eyes filled with loathing.

"Please," said Rura. "Please, Diarmid, no more killing. You and I have already brought destruction upon so many."

"Lassie, would you disarm me? We have a songbird. Let it sing. I wish to know how these Borderers discovered where we live. This was no routine patrol. They do not come so far north at this time of year—unless they already have a target."

"They had their target. A chopper came yesterday and circled over the forest. I think they saw smoke."

"They saw smoke?" He was bewildered.

"I—I didn't put out the fire. It was so chilly, and there

was so little smoke. I thought the embers would keep the house warm until—" She could not go on.

"Why did you not tell me about the chopper?"

"Because—" Rura was crying. "Because I didn't want to leave Lindsays' Haven. I knew that if I told you about the chopper, or if you had seen it, we would have to go away. This house is our home. I—I wanted our child to be born here."

"Rura, the child cannot be born here now. You must know that. You hazarded our lives for a luxury. That was very foolish."

The exterminator spoke. "Rura! Your name is Rura— Rura Alexandra, I think. The graduate with the silver nipple, presumed dead, but actually turned pig-breeder. Big joke!" She began to laugh hysterically.

Diarmid looked down at her. "Rest easy. This is not a song I care to hear."

Garnet laughed louder. "So now you can't screw me before you kill me. The lady sow would not be amused."

"You presume," said Diarmid. "You presume to risk borrowed time."

"I know that death is near," she retorted, "and I do not care to bargain for minutes."

"Well spoken. Not all exterminators are so courageous."

"Evidently the one you have turned into a sow is not!"

"Courage comes in different forms, hellbitch." He raised the laser rifle. "It seems we need not prolong matters."

"Please," sobbed Rura, "*please*. Don't kill her. She can do no more harm."

Diarmid looked at Rura in bewilderment. "Am I to let

her go south with instructions to send up more Borderers for the amusement of Diarmid MacDiarmid?" There was sarcasm in his voice. "Were not she and the dead one out there intent upon our destruction?"

"She can do no more harm," said Rura wearily. "If you let her go on foot without weapons, it will take her a long time to get back to Carlisle—if she is lucky enough to make it. You don't need to kill her, and it costs nothing to give her a small chance of survival."

"This exterminator means something to you?" He was puzzled.

"I just want you to let her live, that's all. You don't need to kill her. Scotland will do it. The world we live in will kill her."

Garnet gave another dreadful laugh. "Tell him how I held you close, dear. Tell him how we kissed. Tell him how I touched you. Tell him you liked it."

"Don't listen to her," said Rura. "Can't you see what she is trying to do?"

Suddenly, Diarmid seemed to relax. "Love, we have more to worry about than the ravings of an exterminator who has run out of time. Do you think there are any other gefcars nearby?"

Rura shook her head. "This is the only one, I'm almost sure. The other hellbitch radioed Carlisle. Carlisle offered to send a chopper in support, but there was no mention of gefcars."

"Did they ask for the chopper?"

"No. They were supposed to call back every two hours."

"Have they done so?"

"No."

"Could you do it?"

"I'd make a mess of it. I don't know their identification code, or even the call procedure."

"The hellbitch can tell us these things."

"She wouldn't."

Diarmid smiled grimly. "That would all depend upon the encouragement she received."

"Diarmid, it is not worth it."

"No? Perhaps you are right. Most likely we would end up stirring the hornets' nest—" He turned to Garnet. "Where is your gefcar?"

"Find it, pig."

He laughed. "I am a free-born man, hellbitch. You, I understand, were manufactured—one way or another. It takes a man and a woman to make people like me. Creatures such as you come from a production line. Well, it will not be too hard to find the gefcar. You had to come by the loch and the valley, and you would not have cared to travel far on foot. Rura, for your sake only, I have been gentle with this hellbitch. While I am gone, gather the things you would take with you. If their gefcar has more fuel than ours, we will use it. When I return, we will burn this house, leaving within it the body of the dead Borderer. And since it is your humor, we will let this one walk south. I doubt that she will walk far."

"We can't burn Lindsays' Haven." Rura was aghast. The house had meant so much.

"We can and will," he said firmly. "Those who come after may just believe that the Borderers accomplished their task. I have given you the life of this creature that meant to kill us. Give me the right to plan for our survival." He held her for a moment and kissed her. "There will be another home where you can bear your child."

170

"There may be another house," she said, "but not another home. This was the one. We have had our chance."

Through the window, she saw that snow was beginning to fall once more.

XXVIII

THE GEFCAR was loaded, the house was burning. The dead Borderer was inside it, the live one lay bound and shivering in the snow.

Rura saw her dreams and hopes going up in smoke. And not only *her* dreams. She thought of the little grave in the forest, marked by seashells and pebbles. . . .

Farewell, Duncan and Jenny, beloved ghosts. Your home was our home. Here we loved and knew happiness, as, perhaps, you loved and knew happiness. But now all our dreams are burning, and the world is dark.

The walls would remain. The rafters were aflame, and the roof would crash in, but the walls would remain. Presently, when the embers had smoldered to death, there would be silence. The heat would dissipate, the snow would cover the ruins. In the spring, moss and lichen and wild flowers would begin their work. As the years passed, the forest would creep closer to Lindsays' Haven, finally engulfing it. The forest would endure, but the forest could not remember.

Diarmid cut the ropes that were binding Garnet. She struggled to her feet, fell down, got up, fell down again, and finally managed to remain standing. Snowflakes fell on her black tunic, remaining despite her body heat.

"So, Borderer," said Diarmid, "you are still alive. I'm sure it amazes us both. If it pleases you to walk south, you are welcome. It is a long way to Carlisle."

Garnet looked at Diarmid and then at Rura, uncomprehending. "What is it?" she asked Rura. "What is it that makes you stay with this—this man? What is it that destroys all your training, all your values, and compels you to accept a way of life that can only end in disaster?"

"I don't know," said Rura. "Call it womanhood. Call it stupidity. I only know that there is no other way of remaining alive."

"Come back with me. We can fix the record. Come back. There is still time."

Rura shook her head. "I'm sorry for you. Truly, I am sorry for you. You don't know, and you will never know."

Diarmid said, "Hellbitch, start moving. One minute from now I shall have lost my patience and my charity."

Garnet looked at him. The hatred had gone from her eyes. It was replaced by incredulity. "If I live, I shall have a story to tell, if anyone will believe it."

"If you can walk across Scotland, you will indeed have a story to tell."

"Won't you give me some food, or a weapon?"

"Is not your life enough?"

"Let her have an emergency pack," pleaded Rura. "That can harm nobody."

"Well, then, give her one. It may last her as far as the Great Glen—unless she meets a hungry Highlander."

Garnet took the emergency pack, in which Rura had managed to conceal a dirk.

"Thank you, Rura Alexandra. I am sorry for many things."

"We are all sorry for many things."

The exterminator turned and walked away, limping a little as the circulation came back painfully into her limbs.

With a great roar and a shower of sparks that became a briefly beautiful fountain in the snow-laden sky, the roof of the house fell in; and the last treasures of Jenny and Duncan Lindsay were consumed.

Rura was too numb, now, to weep. "Where do we go?" she asked.

"North. We could go east, I suppose. It would be better for us, perhaps, but it would also be better for the Borderers—if they pursue the matter. No, we must go north and look for another house. It should not be too difficult. The new gefcar will give us many more kilometers than the old one. Come, Rura. You will feel better when we have found another haven."

She smiled. "It will not be Lindsays' Haven."

"No. It will have its own history, doubtless. And we shall add to it. Have you packed away all that you wish to take?"

"Yes. The necessities. Weapons, food, clothes. Also one or two souvenirs."

"Books?"

She nodded. "Books—and those old letters, and the marriage papers. They seemed to be part of us now. Do you think I'm crazy?"

"No, lassie. It's the world that's crazy." He tried to cheer her up. "There's a place about seventy kilometers to the north, Lochinver. It's on a small sea loch, and on a clear day you can look across the Western Ocean to Lewis and the Outer Hebrides. You'll like Lochinver. In a single day you can walk round twenty freshwater lochs. The

174

trout are as fine as any in Scotland. And there are deer forests, and glens that were fashioned in fairyland. Would you like that?"

She pressed herself close to him. "I would like that very much."

"Then step into the gefcar and we'll lift off. We'll take the sea route. There is little swell, nothing to discomfort us. We can be at Lochinver before the darkness comes."

"Are there any people at Lochinver?"

"I doubt it. But if there are, they will be my people. And so we shall be welcome."

Rura settled herself in the pilot's seat, checked the instruments, started the engines. As the gefcar lifted, she took a last look at Lindsays' Haven. Through the light curtain of snowflakes she saw a funeral pyre. Dead dreams were burning.

Then she swung the gefcar round and headed down an avenue of pine trees towards the sea.

XXIX

LOCHINVER WAS all that Diarmid had promised—a beautiful, desolate little place. A cluster of derelict houses, no sign of life.

They came in from the sea an hour before dusk and swept up the loch. No one shot at them. There was no movement on shore. Even the snow had stopped. There was only the sound of the sea and the bleak Scottish twilight.

Rura grounded the gefcar on what had once been the main street, and got out. She shivered in the cold still air and gazed at the ruins of houses and a few larger buildings, antiseptically beautiful under a thin covering of snow. The scene was immensely sad. Here, centuries ago, there had been a thriving little community. She tried to imagine it as it once might have been on a late autumn evening long ago. Lights in the cottage windows, smoke rising from chimneys, children stealing a few last minutes of play before bedtime, perhaps the sound of merriment from a tavern, women completing their day's tasks before an hour or two of relaxation and then sleeping in warm beds and in the arms of their men. Lovers holding each other close by starlight. Perhaps a dog howling at the moon. . . .

Diarmid stood beside her, an arm round her shoulders, sensing her thoughts. "It was once a very innocent world," he said. "Our ancestors had their problems, no doubt, but they were secure in the natural order of things. Men and women fitted well together in those days. They would not have believed in the nightmare that could follow. I'm going to look for a cottage with a roof—or part of a roof—and a fireplace. Get back into the gefcar, Rura, and stay warm."

"I want to be with you."

"That is my pleasure also."

They found a cottage with a roof. It had no doors or windows, but it had a roof and a hearth.

"Bring food and blankets," said Diarmid. "I'll find some wood. Tonight we'll have a great fire. We'll roast ourselves and eat our fill and sleep like the dead. Tomorrow we'll work inland and find a house that shall be all you want."

"I had the house that was all I wanted."

"There are others. Scotland is not yet so poor that it cannot shelter its own."

Diarmid found timbers that were snow-covered and rotten with age. It was easier to break them than to cut them; but they burned well. They crackled and hissed and sent sparks up the chimney, and gave the derelict cottage a semblance of life. The rats, unaccustomed to such noise and heat, scurried away. Rura cooked venison and mushrooms and apples. The food tasted good.

Presently, they slept—fully clothed, in front of the dying fire, covered in tattered blankets, lying on sheepskins.

At first light, Diarmid rose, stretched himself. "Today," he promised, "I will find you a house that you will like."

She didn't believe him. But, oddly, he found it.

177

It was a very small house, two tiny rooms only. There was no door to it. Nor was there a cellar; and the windows were only gaping holes. But the roof and walls were sound, and the stone floor was not too badly cracked. Something could be made of it. It was not like Lindsays' Haven, redolent of the past, with contents that gave it some identity. It was just a bare stone cottage that had managed to survive. Probably it had once been a keeper's home. It nestled in a forest as Lindsays' Haven had. And it was no more than four or five kilometers from the sea.

Diarmid killed a number of totally surprised rats and lighted a fire that was hot enough and noisy enough to drive the rest of the wildlife back into the forest. Rura transferred the things she had brought in the gefcar to the cottage. Weapons, clothes, food—and the luxury of a few books and some brittle pieces of paper.

Skins would have to cover the window holes at night, and skins would have to be hung over the doorway, until Diarmid could make something. This place would have to be called MacDiarmid's Promise, she decided. It had no history.

A thaw came and the snow melted rapidly. The thaw made the forest smell wonderful, made it smell of life. Rura's spirits began to rise. Diarmid was right. Home was the place that you could make into home. Soon she would explore the forest and the coast, and soon she would be at home.

Rura spent the rest of the daylight hours making the cottage as comfortable as possible. It was surprising what you could do with a few deerskins and sheepskins. There was no furniture. All that had disappeared—looted or burned, most likely—long ago. But there was plenty of wood; and Diarmid had his dirk and an ancient axe and an even more ancient handsaw. In time he would contrive something. Meanwhile, they would sleep on skins over a mattress of heather and dry grass, and eat sitting on the floor. It was no great hardship.

While there was still some light left, Diarmid went fishing in the nearest loch. He was not gone long; and when he returned, he had half a dozen brown trout. Hunger, at least, would not be an immediate threat. The small lochs abounded in fish; and he had seen several deer.

As Rura cooked the evening meal, she began to feel more cheerful. The wind whistled through the temporary coverings on the doorway and windows; but there was an immense fire, and the cottage was warm.

The Republic of Anglia, London, the world of women, the fraternity of exterminators, Curie Milford's fanatical zeal—all that was very far away. Diarmid seemed confident that the exterminators would not venture so far north at this time of the year. Rura was content to accept his judgement. She was beginning to feel secure again. In the spring her baby would be born. In the spring Diarmid intended to either raise another fighting force or to join someone else's band of guerillas. It was a hopeless cause, Rura knew. The fighting resources of the Republic of Anglia were far greater than Diarmid imagined. The comparatively few free men of Scotland could never hope to inflict any serious damage on the Republic. All they could hope for was that Curie Milford might decide that it was too costly to annihilate them completely. A slender hope. Curie Milford had an unswerving hatred of men.

Still, the spring seemed very far away. Rura would be thankful for a peaceful winter—a few months in which she could enjoy the illusion that the Northwest Highlands were a private sanctuary. A few months during which she could enjoy discovering what it was like to belong to a man. To be a sex object, something possessed. To be a fulfilled woman, something to be cherished and protected.

Such a small ambition—but still too great to be realized. . . .

She slept well in Diarmid's arms. He murmured in his sleep, and held her fiercely. She caught the word Flora, but it did not matter. This was for Flora also, and for Ewan. Once, when Diarmid became agitated, she opened her eyes and studied his face by the dying firelight. Such an old face, lined, weatherbeaten, sad. Yet, also, such a young face lying under the marks of time.

Morning came. They breakfasted. Diarmid went out to hunt deer. Another supply of meat would have to be established against the freezing weeks when hunting would be almost impossible.

It was a fine, clear morning. Frosty but not freezing. Rura decided that she, too, would go hunting. Not with crossbow, but with a laser rifle. This time, if she saw a great stag, she would kill it. She would discipline herself not to indulge in spiritual luxuries.

Diarmid had been gone perhaps an hour before Rura was ready to set out. She had the fully charged rifle that had belonged to Garnet. She wondered how Garnet was faring on her walk south. Guiltily, Rura hoped that Garnet would make it.

It was late in the morning when Rura left the cottage. She had barely gone a hundred meters into the forest when she heard the chopper.

It circled the cottage twice, then it turned south. For a time, Rura was frozen with fear and disbelief. This was no accident. The chopper knew exactly where to look.

Rura ran to the gefcar, as yet uncamouflaged, but hidden under pine trees. The transceiver was switched off, as she knew it would be. But under the standard transceiver there was a little black box, and a wire led from it to the gefcar's aerial.

So that was it! An automatic transmitter! Rura switched on the receiver and traversed the wavebands. She got the gefcar's bleep, bleep, loud and clear on high frequency.

Instantly, she lasered the black box. But the damage was already done. This time Diarmid had seen the chopper also. He came hurrying back to the cottage.

"It was the gefcar," explained Rura. "It had an automatic transmitter sending out bleeps for their direction-finders. I'm sorry. I ought to have checked it."

Diarmid looked depressed. "I should have expected something like that. They have been losing too many recently. You have destroyed it?"

"Yes. But the damage is done. They can pinpoint us."

Diarmid looked at the sky. A short time ago, he had been exulting in the fine weather. Now he hated it.

"The chopper will be back," he said, "probably this afternoon, spotting for a string of exterminators."

"What shall we do?" But Rura already knew what they would have to do. Trying to make the cottage seem like a home had been only a sad waste of time. With dreadful clarity she knew it would always be like that. Wherever they were, sooner or later the exterminators would come.

"Pack everything we need," said Diarmid. "Then we will move the gefcar about a kilometer nearer the sea. We must find a place where it can be reasonably well hidden, but where there is a clear run to the water at maximum speed."

"You don't want to leave now?"

"No, Rura. For the sake of others in the Highlands, I want to demonstrate to the hellbitches that operations this far from Carlisle can be expensive."

It did not take long to load the gefcar. Diarmid found a place to park it in a cluster of pine trees near the edge of the forest. There was a clear run to Lochinver and the open water. When this had been accomplished, they went back to the cottage, each carrying a couple of laser rifles. They went back to the cottage to wait.

Diarmid kindled a fire. This time, the advertisement was deliberate. They cooked trout and watched the sun slide across the sky. The air had become warm, the sunlight softly golden. More Indian Summer.

After they had eaten, they lay close together on a sheepskin, outside the cottage, basking in a luxury that could not last.

"Why do you stay with me? Why do you love me?" asked Diarmid, stroking her hair.

"Because," Rura floundered. "Because you are a man, I suppose. . . . I don't know. There must be many reasons. Perhaps the chopper will not come back."

"It will come," he said. "It will come."

They made love. It was a good thing to do, reflected Rura, when death was near. It would be much easier to die if one had made love.

The chopper was considerate. It allowed them to make love, to caress each other, to doze a little before it came droning in from the south.

Diarmid heard it first. He sprang to his feet and snatched a laser rifle.

"Quick! Into the cottage. Let them see no movement. Let us tempt them."

"Tempt them to do what?"

"Come lower, be inquisitive. If we can take out the spotter, there is a chance we can shake off its earth-bound friends. I don't think it will be spotting for a single gefcar this time."

They were inside the cottage, peeping through the windows, long before the chopper arrived. It came in high, well out of laser range, and hovered right over the house. Diarmid cursed. It did not seem as if it would be tempted to inspect more closely. Probably it was just going to sit in the sky until the exterminators came.

"We'll have to make a run for it," said Rura anxiously. "The gefcars can't be more than three or four minutes away."

Diarmid was silent for a moment or two, staring grimly at the inaccessible machine. "So it won't play. Then we'll make it play. Rura, I'm going to make a dash for it —but not too quickly, if I'm to draw them. I'll limp as if I'm wounded, and I'll just carry my crossbow. They have good glasses. They'll see a Highland pig all set up for the burning. They'll want to hit me before I can get really good tree cover. So they will have to come down fast. Wait till you are absolutely sure before you laser them. If you don't knock it out of the sky first beaming, there won't be another chance."

"Diarmid, don't! Please don't! Let us try to draw them together."

"With laser rifles in our hands? They will sit tight. And if we don't have the rifles, they will get us both. Rura, do as I say—and be sure."

He snatched his crossbow and stepped out of the doorway into the clearing. He appeared to look around him uncertainly for a moment or two, then he began to limp away, dragging one leg badly.

They won't take the bait, thought Rura. *The chopper will tell the gefcars and let them run him down.*

But the chopper took the bait after a brief hesitation. Its engines whined, and it came dropping fast. A gout of flame sprang up from the ground behind Diarmid. Then another burst of flame just ahead.

Rura stared, white-faced, through the window. Its lasers would kill Diarmid; but it was not yet low enough for Rura to laser through metal and destroy the chopper's controls.

Diarmid went faster, weaving from side to side, tongues of flame leaping up all around him. His jacket was smoldering. There was a lick of flame on his trews. The ground exploded into flame right in front of him. He fell, rolling over, his clothes on fire.

Rura screamed—and had just enough sense to tear her gaze away from the writhing figure and look at the chopper. Maybe it was in range, maybe it wasn't. But she couldn't let Diarmid burn like that. She ran out of the house towards him. He saw her.

"Now!" he screamed. "Damn you, now!"

She raised the rifle, maximum range, narrow field, maximum burn. It was all automatic. It was all slow motion. It was all high speed. It was all nightmare.

She could see the chopper pilot's head. She could see two of the crew with rifles, sweeping away at the ground below, intent on turning it into an inferno. They had spotted her. The rifles swung towards her.

Then the chopper's engines coughed, and smoke came from its vulnerable nose. It whirled crazily, writhing strange smoke signs in the sky. Something fell out of it—was it a body? Rura no longer cared. She raced to Diarmid, tore off her jacket, flung it on top of him, smothered the flames. He coughed and groaned and writhed.

Somewhere above, metal screamed through the sky. About a hundred and fifty meters away, the stricken chopper fell into the forest. There was a great tearing, then silence, then a dull whoof, followed by a mushroom of fire.

XXX

THE LEGS of Diarmid's trews were almost burned away. Some of the charred fabrics came off easily; but patches stuck to his flesh. Rura did not dare pull at them for fear of what she would find underneath. The upper part of his body had not fared so badly as his legs; but one arm hung limp in a smoldering sleeve. She tried to tear the cloth away.

"No time to make me pretty," he gasped. "Get us to the gefcar. The hellbitches will be all over us if we don't move quickly."

She managed to get him to his feet. He whimpered, then stifled the whimper. She put his good arm around her shoulder and took as much of his weight as she could.

"There are painkillers in the gefcar, Diarmid."

"I know. I'll need them. Rura, I am still the laird. If I fall, if I faint, you are to go on. That is a command. No matter—no matter what you may think, you carry my child. You will save the child."

"Yes, Diarmid. I understand." She would have agreed to anything—anything that he wanted.

Now they were among the trees, tottering slowly from side to side, but making some progress. Diarmid's face was twisted with pain. His eyes were glazed, as if he could not focus. But his mind remained clear. "It has been a good run, Rura. The hellbitches will remember us. Thank you for teaching me to read."

Rura heard a gefcar. She flung Diarmid down in the wet, mercifully cool bracken, and lay almost on top of him, hiding her face, expecting at any moment to feel a laser beam burn them both into oblivion.

The gefcar came slowly, weaving between the trees. It came very close, but not close enough. Perhaps its crew was concentrating on finding the chopper. When it had gone away, Rura stood up. She tried to lift Diarmid, but he was unconscious. She wept with fear and frustration. Then she slapped his face hard. It had no effect. She shook him. In desperation, she kicked him. He groaned and opened his eyes.

"Stand up!" She tried to help him, but he was too heavy. "Stand up, Diarmid, please." No response.

She kicked him again. "Stand up, you filthy Highland pig! Can't you take a little rough treatment, snout-face? I thought you presumed to be a man!"

Diarmid gave a roar of anger, and managed to get to his knees.

"Not good enough, pig. Try harder."

Somehow she got him to his feet. Somehow, with her arm around him, they continued their drunkards' walk.

Rura heard the sound of another gefcar. Once more, she flung Diarmid into the wet bracken. Once more the gefcar passed by—not quite so close this time.

She tried to make him wake again. She slapped and kicked. Finally, she bit his lip. She kissed him and saw her tears fall on his face. Then she bit his lip with animal savagery.

"Get up, pig! Walk, damn you! Call yourself a man! You make me vomit."

He clawed at her, pulled himself up.

"March, pig. Flora would laugh at you. Ewan would hide his head in shame."

Diarmid tried to speak, but the words only gurgled in his throat. Once more the drunkards' walk.

But the place where the gefcar was hidden was now in sight. Rura recognized it. She let Diarmid go, and he fell. Then she raced to the gefcar, started the engines and brought the machine close.

"Stop groveling, scum. Must I do all the work?"

He gazed up at her, uncomprehending.

"Pig, you've had it! You are weaker than a woman. I've wasted my time."

Diarmid let out a great cry—and leaped to his feet.

"I'll see you in hell," he said thickly. "I'll see you in hell."

Somehow she tumbled him into the gefcar. Then she took the controls, lifted and raced for Lochinver and the open sea.

XXXI

It was already late in the afternoon as the gefcar swept out to sea. There was a gentle swell, easy to ride on maximum lift. Thirty kilometers away to the west, the hills of Lewis were low ghostly shapes. The sun moved inexorably towards them, as if it would disperse the insubstantial contours with a touch of fire.

Diarmid slumped in his seat, conscious but unmoving. He stared dully at nothing. The air-conditioner was working full blast, but the gefcar was filled with the smell of burnt clothes and burnt flesh. It was the most terrible smell in the world.

Rura fought down the nausea and forced herself to think. Could she afford the time to cross thirty kilometers of water? She could not. Diarmid needed painkillers and dressings. Besides, if there were another chopper near the coast, the wake of a gefcar would stand out like a carved white furrow.

She decided to swing north, hugging the coast. She would find a small bay, not more than about ten kilometers away; and then she would find some kind of cover and touch down.

She was lucky. She rounded a headland and found a tiny cove, silvery sand, accessible beach, moderately high cliffs. She took the gefcar close under the cliffs and cut the engines. She fumbled in the medikit and found the pain shots. She put one shot into Diarmid's good arm and one in the shoulder of the burt arm. Then, for good measure, she put a shot in the top of each of his legs.

Four shots ought to have knocked him cold. But he barely seemed to notice them. Surprisingly, he became lucid.

"So you got us away from the hellbitches. The age of miracles has not passed. Where are we?"

"I don't know. About ten or twelve kilometers north of Lochinver. We came round a great headland."

"Ah, that would be Point of Stoer, no doubt. How do we look from the sky?"

"I think we would be hard to see. The cliffs give good cover from the south, and the top of the gefcar is about the same color as the sand. Diarmid, how do you feel?"

He managed a faint smile. "I think I would wish to avoid hand-to-hand fighting at this moment. Don't fret, lassie, I'm only parboiled."

"I'll have to put dressings on your burns."

"Aye, you will. I seem to recollect that you called me pig, snout-face, scum."

"Diarmid, I'm sorry. I—I had to do something."

He turned his head to her. Some of his hair had been burned. His eyes were bloodshot. One of his cheekbones was grazed raw. There were streaks where tears had washed over the ash on his skin. His lip was swollen and bloody where she had bitten him. He looked terrible. He looked very much a man.

"So. I have made a Highland woman of you. That is something. I am content."

She kissed his forehead very tenderly. "Diarmid, I'm

going to lay a blanket on the sand. If you can lie down on it, I'll cut the burnt clothing away and put dressings on your legs."

"It is a fine afternoon," he said. "I've a mind to bathe in the sun. The hurt is going away, and I feel almost human."

"I gave you some shots."

"Ah, so that is what it was."

"They are supposed to make you sleepy."

"I'm not sleepy at all. Maybe it will come later." He laughed grimly. "I was told that my father was a strong and stubborn man. Maybe he has given me these qualities. He had little else to give."

"Can you stand? Can you get out of the gefcar?"

"Call me a filthy Highland pig, and see."

Rura took skins and an old blanket and laid them on the dry sand in the lee of a large boulder. Diarmid stepped groggily out of the gefcar, tottered to the skins and gratefully lay down. The air was warm, beautifully warm. The sand glistened in the rich gold light of the lowering sun.

Rura went to work with the medikit. The extent of the burns was no worse than she had feared. Great strips of flesh peeled away with the charred clothing. She sprayed the antiseptic aerosol over his legs, then smeared on the antibiotic cream and bound the worst afflicted parts gently. Then she dealt with the burnt, now withered, arm and the great raw patch on his chest. If Diarmid could have been given skilled treatment in a hospital in the Republic of Anglia, he would have been as good as new in ten days. But if he was allowed to remain in the Northwest Highlands, without adequate treatment, food or shelter, he was a dying man.

He was a dying man. That much she knew. That much she would have to learn to accept. The knowledge put her beyond tears.

The pain shots had done their work marvelously. Diarmid did not complain when the burnt flesh was torn away from his body, when the blood oozed from cauterized veins. He was more interested in the world about him.

"I never realized," he said, "how much I love the sound of the sea. Men come and go, but the sea remains. It is the cradle of life. I was told once that all living things came out of the sea. When humankind has passed from the earth, the sea will still bring forth new life. There is endurance for you."

"You must rest now," said Rura. "You must take a little rest."

He smiled. "Rest. There will be plenty of that soon enough. We must make plans, Rura. You carry my child."

The air was still warm, but the wind had strengthened. Not many meters from where Diarmid lay, small breakers were carving new and transient patterns in the sand.

"We will find another home," said Rura. "You will get well and hunt deer and fish and salmon and trout."

Diarmid raised himself up and gazed at the sea. "Men come and go, but the sea remains. . . . We took out their chopper, did we not?"

"Yes, we took out their chopper."

"Rura, I want you to go back. Listen carefully to what I have to say. I want you to go back. If you say the right things—if you do the right things—they will welcome you. They may let you bear the child. If—"

"If what?"

"If you take back the body of Diarmid MacDiarmid."

For a time, Rura did not speak. There was nothing but

192

the sound of the waves, the steady, muted murmur of the wind.

At least she said, "I love you and I will lie beside you, in life or in death. There is nothing more to say, Diarmid. That is how it is."

"So!" he gave a great sigh. "So the little exterminator presumes upon my injuries."

"I am a Highland woman," retorted Rura. "I care for my man."

For a while she sat beside him, holding his hand, neither of them speaking. Diarmid lay on his back, moving his head a little, gazing at sea and rocks and sky. He seemed utterly fascinated by what he saw, as if he were seeing it for the first time.

"I think I would like to be a rock," he said at length, "a great rock on the Scottish coast. If a rock could know that it was a rock, that is. I would endure for a hundred thousand years, with the sea drubbing me and wearing a little away each year, with the wind singing about me, with snow and ice in winter and the heat of the sun in summer. Aye, it would be a good thing to be a rock, with the seals playing and the sea birds calling long after the race of man has gone."

Rura said, "Diarmid, what shall we do? Tell me what we must do!"

He did not seem to hear her. "Yes, it was a terrible thing to set women against men, men against women. United, we might have stood. We made terrible mistakes; but, united, we might have stood. Divided, men and women shall surely fall. Not all your cloning or parthenogenesis can breed a race strong enough to build a civilization that will survive."

"Diarmid, please tell me what to do."

"Ah, yes." A frown of concentration came over his face. "What to do. . . . It will be a frosty night. Maybe more snow. What to do . . . .We have no refuge, nor is there—" He stopped, listening.

A faint throbbing, now louder. The unmistakable, dreadful sound of a chopper. It came slowly over the sea, obviously searching the coast. Rura dragged Diarmid behind a boulder. There was no time to get the skins and the blanket; but probably they would not appear to be much from the air.

The chopper swung in from the sea, directly towards them. It could hardly fail to see them; but, incredibly, it didn't see them. It passed inland, and the sound of the engines died.

Diarmid was perplexed. "I can't understand it. Such activity so far north at this time of the year. This is something new. What can have caused it?"

"Perhaps Diarmid MacDiarmid caused it," said Rura. "This summer you have managed to give the Border Regiment much to remember."

He smiled. "I had forgotten. Already it seems so long ago. What to do. . . . What else is there to do but go further north? We shall sleep in the gefcar this night, Rura. Tomorrow I will be stronger. Tomorrow I will be intelligent. Tomorrow I will find a home where you can tend me."

Rura dreaded the thought of tomorrow. If only one could laser the mainspring in the clock of time.

"This is your country, Diarmid. I am a stranger. How much further north can we go?"

"Fifty, sixty kilometers, perhaps. That takes us to Cape Wrath, the end of the world, Rura, wild, desolate, beautiful. Cliffs rising three hundred meters sheer from the sea. A bleak country . . . the end of the world. Perhaps beyond the reach of these vicious metal flies that buzz through the peaceful sky."

"Can you get into the gefcar?"

"Rura, you have done wonderful work upon me. There is no pain, only a little lightness, as if I had taken whiskey."

But he could not stand alone, and the breath rattled painfully in his lungs as he tried to haul himself into the gefcar.

"Shall I follow the coast?"

"No, lassie. Lift inland. Darkness comes fast as we travel north. I would not wish to be caught between the ocean and a wall of rock."

The sun was very low over the sea as Rura lifted off. Low and dull red. There might still be an hour of daylight left. Perhaps a little more.

She looked at the sun and the sea for a moment, savoring the desolate splendor. Then she swung along the beach, seeking an easy route inland.

XXXII

IT SNOWED during the night; not heavily, but enough to silt up on the windows of the gefcar. Rura had kept the air-conditioner going all the time, but the battery was failing and there was not much heat.

For the first part of the night, Diarmid rested, hardly moving, his breathing shallow but even. In the early hours of the morning the fever came. He jerked and twisted on the seat that had been lowered back so that it was almost a couch. He jerked and twisted, and cried and spoke in a language she could not understand. The dead language of Gaelic, she supposed. Perhaps he had learned a little as a child.

When he shivered, she held the sheepskin close around him. When he burned, she loosened his clothes and switched the fan to full blast.

The gefcar was on a promontory at Cape Wrath. Diarmid was right. It was the end of the world. There was nothing outside but snow and moorland, and great cliffs reaching down through the blackness to the sea.

My man is dying, she thought dully, *and there is nothing I can do for him. Yes, there is something I can do for him. I can commit his body to the sea and pray that he is transformed into a great rock that will lie forever on some Scottish beach while the seasons fly like seconds, and while birds wheel across all the summer mornings that are left in time. And then, like an animal, I can seek some lair that will keep me through the winter. And in the spring I can bring forth a manchild. These things are all that I can do for him. They will have to be enough.*

A little before dawn, the fever seemed to go. It went very quickly, leaving Diarmid abnormally cool. He woke. There was some pain in his legs, but not too much.

"Where are we, Rura?"

"Cape Wrath. You told me to get us here."

"Did I? So I did. A wise decision. Cape Wrath is a long way from Carlisle, nearly as far in Scotland as you can get. It has been snowing. You look tired. Have I been much trouble?"

"I am not tired," she lied, "and you have been little trouble."

"How old are you?"

"Twenty."

"I am sorry."

"Why are you sorry?"

"Because I am nearly twice your age, Rura. I have seen more summers, I have endured more winters. I have more memories. I am sorry."

"There is no cause to be sorry. In the spring, I will give you a son. That should age me somewhat. The son of Diarmid MacDiarmid is bound to be troublesome."

"Rura, we love each other. Strange, is it not? The exterminator and the Highland pig. We love each other, and so we must not cheat. I am dying. You know that."

"Yes, I know it."

"Mine is the easy task," said Diarmid. "I know that also. But it would please me—yes, it would please me if you were to make a serious attempt to live. Have you the stomach for it?"

She smiled and patted her belly. "As you can see, I have the stomach for it."

"Good. Listen carefully. I will not delay you long, Rura. Afterwards, I would wish you to make for the east coast and work cautiously south. Try to find a Highland man or a fighting unit. They will need women, they will need children. You understand?"

"I understand. It shall be as you wish. I will do all I can to ensure that the child lives."

"Good, then. There is no more to be said about that. The sun is rising, Rura. If there were not snow on these damned windows, I could watch it rise."

Rura got out of the gefcar and scraped the snow away with her fingernails. Diarmid watched the sun rise. A large red sun. He watched it greedily, drinking every moment as one who had never seen it before or would never see it again.

"Tell the child about me. Tell him all that you know. Tell him I was a man. It will be enough."

"I will tell him."

"Tell him also that love comes rarely. Tell him that his father was twice blessed."

For a time, Rura and Diarmid lay together in the gefcar. The pain had gone completely now, but he could only move one arm. He used it to good advantage. He stroked Rura's hair, he felt the contours of her face, he put his hand on the promise of life in her belly.

After a time, he became thirsty. Rura went out of the gefcar to gather snow and make him a drink. She was surprised to see that the sun was quite high now. Time had passed so quickly. It was near to midday.

She was scraping snow into a small pan when she heard the chopper. It came from the south. It came low, very low. There was no possibility that it would not see the gefcar, exposed on moorland by the cliffs.

The chopper saw it, circled, hovered, dropped something.

The gefcar exploded. Rura ran towards the wreckage.

Diarmid had been blown clear. But he was dead. He lay in the snow with his eyes closed. and a look of astonishment on his face.

Rura cradled him in her arms, whispered words that he would never hear. One part of her was aware of sounds, aware of happenings. She knew that the chopper had touched down. She knew that someone was coming towards her. It did not matter. Diarmid was dead. She nursed him and rocked him and whispered words of great tenderness.

"Well, sow. It has been a long chase. Was it worth it for the pig that lies in the snow?"

Rura felt the dirk in her hand. The dirk she had learned to carry as a Highland woman. She rose up and faced the exterminator. The exterminator armed with a laser rifle and the authority of Curie Milford's Republic of Anglia.

"Yes, hellbitch, it was worth it."

"Rura!"

In the moment that it took Lieutenant Kayt to absorb the fact, Rura thrust the dirk into her breast.

Kayt stood there swaying, amazed.

"Rura!"

"Rura MacDiarmid, hellbitch. My name is Rura Mac-Diarmid."

Kayt's knees buckled. She sank down into the snow. "Rura," she gasped. "I loved you . . . I loved you!"

Rura did not hear, did not care to hear. Kayt mumbled and groaned and turned the snow red.

Someone else came out of the chopper. There was another laser rifle to worry about. But Rura was past worrying.

She held Diarmid. She held him close. She whispered tender words. She said: "I will love you until—"

And then there was darkness. The darkness of forever.

11
NOVELS BY
ROBERT A. HEINLEIN

055004	Between Planets 95c
106005	Citizen of the Galaxy 95c
318006	Have Space Suit-Will Travel 95c
711408	Red Planet 95c
733303	Rocket Ship Galileo 95c
734400	The Rolling Stones 95c
777300	Space Cadet 95c
780007	The Star Beast 95c
811257	Time for the Stars 95c
826602	Tunnel in the Sky 95c
915025	The Worlds of Robert A. Heinlein 95c

Available wherever paperbacks are sold or use this coupon.

- -

Frank Herbert

172619 Dune $1.25

302612 Green Brain 60c

909267 The Worlds of Frank Herbert 95c

URSULA LEGUIN

107011 City of Illusion 60c

478008 Left Hand of Darkness 95c

669523 Planet of Exile 75c

732917 Rocannon's World 75c

Samuel R. Delany

045914 Babel 17 95c

047225 Ballad of Beta 2 60c

196816 Einstein Intersection 95c

226415 Fall of the Towers $1.25

390211 Jewels of Aptor 75c

Available wherever paperbacks are sold or use this coupon.

A. E. Van Vogt

048603	The Battle of Forever	95c
104109	Children of Tomorrow	95c
137984	Darkness on Diamondia	95c
228114	The Far Out Worlds of A. E. Van Vogt	75c
697003	Quest For the Future	95c
765008	The Silkie	60c
871814	The War Against the Rulls	$1.25
878553	The Weapon Shops of Isher	60c

JOHN BRUNNER

033001	The Atlantic Abomination	60c
166686	Dramaturges of Yan	75c
381210	Jagged Orbit	$1.25
524009	Meeting at Infinity	60c
812701	Times Without Number	60c
822106	Traveler in Black	75c

Available wherever paperbacks are sold or use this coupon.

Great Science Fiction Collections.

Science Fiction
THE GREAT YEARS!

The World's Best
Award-Winning Science Fiction
Comes from Ace

029363 **Armageddon 2419 A.D.** Nowlan 75c

061770 **The Big Show** Laumer 75c

067017 **The Black Star Passes** Campbell 75c

136002 **The Dancers of Noyo** St. Clair 95c

279059 **Gender Genocide** Cooper 95c

371005 **Interplanetary Hunter** Barnes 95c

489708 **Looking Backward From the Year 2,000**
Reynolds 95c

516559 **Falling Astronauts** Malzberg 75c

524603 **The Men and the Mirror**
Rocklynne 95c

623801 **The Omega Point** Zebrowski 75c

635904 **Operation Umanaq** Rankin 75c

734384 **Roller Coaster World** Bulmer 75c

816561 **Tomorrow Lies in Ambush** Shaw 95c

861807 **Veruchia** Tubb 95c

876011 **Warlord of the Air** Moorcock 75c

Available wherever paperbacks are sold or use this coupon.

ACE SCIENCE FICTION DOUBLES
Two books back-to-back
Just 95c each

009902 **Against Arcturus** Putney
Time Thieves Rackham

102939 **The Chariots of Ra** Bulmer
Earth Strings Rackham

116509 **Computer War**
Code Duello Reynolds

156976 **The Unteleported Man**
Dr. Futurity Dick

317552 **The Hard Way Up** Chandler
Veiled World Lory

370627 **The Inheritors**
The Gateway to Never Chandler

534156 **Mr. Justice** Piserchia
Heirarchies Phillifent

665257 **Pirates of Zan**
Mutant Weapon Leinster

763805 **Silent Invaders** Silverberg
Battle of Venus Temple

769604 **The Sky is Falling**
Badge of Infamy del Rey

775254 **Son of the Tree**
House of Iszm Vance

799759 **Technos**
A Scatter of Sardust Tubb

939009 **A Yank at Valhalla** Hamilton
The Sun Destroyers Rocklynne

Available wherever paperbacks are sold or use this coupon.

---

ace books, (Dept. MM) Box 576, Times Square Station
New York, N.Y. 10036
Please send me titles checked above.

I enclose $ . . . . Add 15¢ handling fee per copy.

Name . . . .

Address . . . .

City . . . . State . . . . Zip . . . .
Please allow 4 weeks for delivery.   12-72-8D

WINNER OF
THE HUGO AWARD
AND THE
NEBULA AWARD
FOR BEST
SCIENCE FICTION
NOVEL OF
THE YEAR

045922	Babel 17	Delaney	95c
062190	Big Time	Leiber	95c
106229	City	Simak	95c
166413	Dragon Masters Vance The Last Castle	Vance	95c
167023	Dream Master	Zelazny	95c
172619	Dune	Herbert	$1.25
196824	Einstein Intersection	Delany	95c
249011	Four for Tomorrow	Zelazny	95c
478008	Left Hand of Darkness	LeGuin	95c
727826	Rite of Passage	Panshin	95c
806927	This Immortal	Zelazny	95c

Available wherever paperbacks are sold or use this coupon.